MW00945656

Nick Newton
IS NOT A GENIUS

S. E. M. Ishida

journeyforth®
Greenville, South Carolina

Library of Congress Cataloging-in Publication Data

Names: Ishida, S. E. M., 1990–
Title: Nick Newton is not a genius / S.E.M. Ishida.
Description: Greenville, South Carolina : JourneyForth Books, [2016] |
Summary: “Nick Newton finds metal parts in a box in the attic along with notes from his late grandfather that once assembled lead Nick’s family on adventure until Nick solves a mystery”—Provided by pub lisher.
Identifiers: LCCN 2016008087 (print) | LCCN 2016022997 (ebook) |
ISBN 9781628562354 (perfect bound pbk. : alk. paper) | ISBN 9781628562361 (ebook)
Subjects: | CYAC: Inventions—Fiction. | Family life—Fiction. |
Genius—Fiction.
Classification: LCC PZ7.1.I87 Ni 2016 (print) | LCC PZ7.1.I87 (ebook) |
DDC
[Fic]—dc23
LC record available at https://lccn.loc.gov/2016008087

Illustrator: Dana Thompson
Designer: Craig Oesterling
Page layout: Michael Boone

Greenville, South Carolina 29614

JourneyForth Books is a division of BJU Press.

Printed in the United States of America

ISBN 978-1-62856-235-4
eISBN 978-1-62856-236-1

15 14 13 12 11 10 9 8 7 6 5 4 3 2 1

To Mom and Dad

Thanks for all the stories.

Part One

Part Two

Part Three

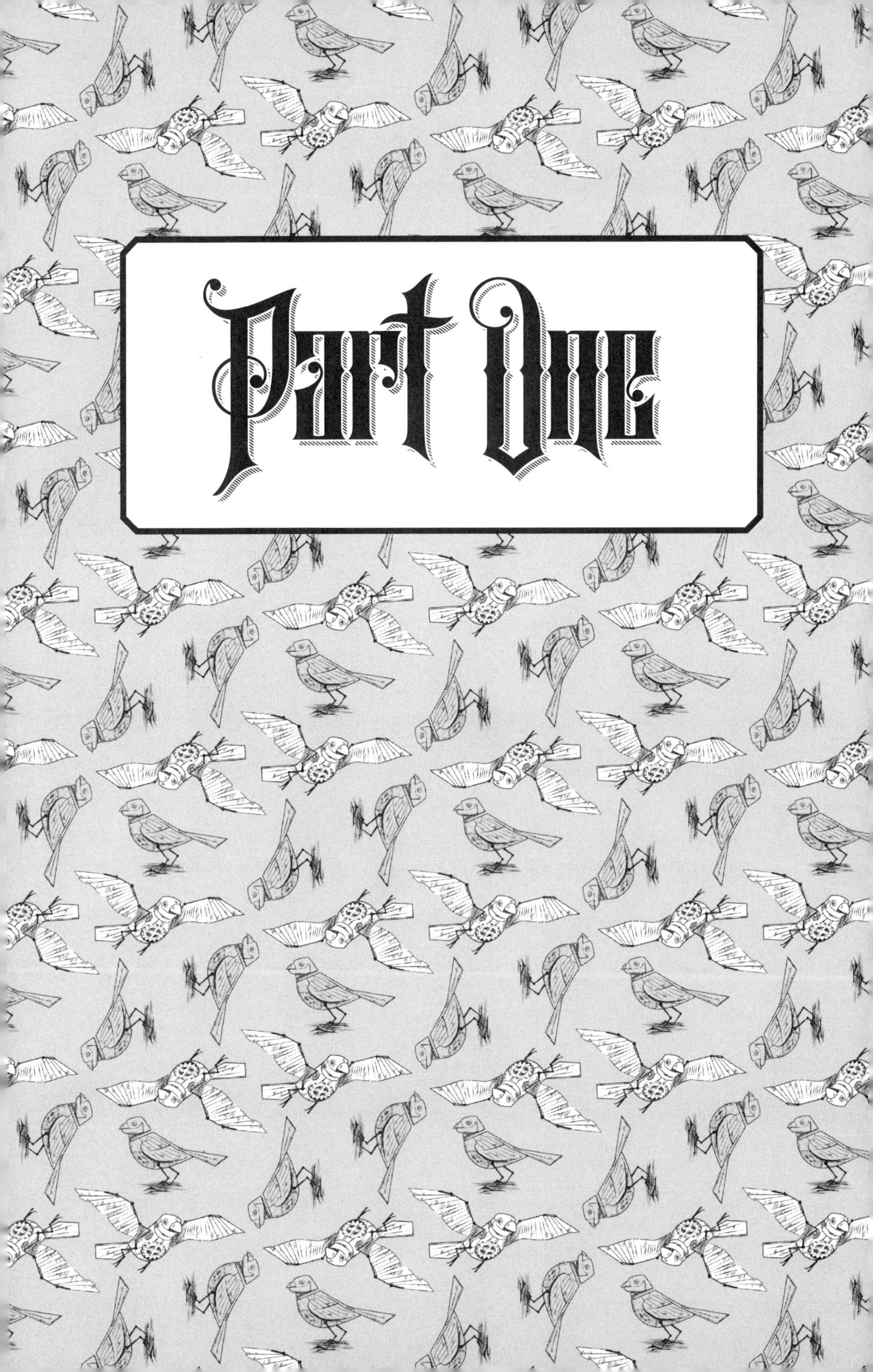

Part One

1 A STROKE OF GENIUS

The headmaster slowly pulled papers from the envelope on his desk. My feet dangled from the leather chair. Mom sat in a matching chair next to me. As usual, Dad sat in his wheelchair.

The headmaster presented the papers to Dad. "I am sorry, Mr. and Dr. Newton. Nicholas's test scores were merely average for a child in the country of Thauma."

My parents' expressions did not change. Mine didn't either. I already knew I wasn't a genius. I looked at Dad. He's a genius. He's been drawing since he could hold a crayon, and he began writing music before he could read.

I looked at Mom. She's a genius too. She discovered a new type of butterfly when she was just a toddler. The butterfly she found is named after her.

I thought of my older sister Erma. She is a genius at everything. Or at least she tries to be. She does very well at trying to be.

I thought of my baby sister Addie. Mom and Dad say it's still too early to tell if she's a genius. Erma says a genius wouldn't drool so much. I, however, think that Addie *is* a genius. I've heard her babble out Morse code when she's hungry. She also stacks her toys in groups of prime numbers.

I had lost track of the conversation.

"But Nick's science fair project," Mom told the headmaster. "Surely his research on cuttlefish was worth something."

"Nick failed to communicate with the cuttlefish," the headmaster said dryly, "because he failed to keep them alive."

I thought about my fourth grade science fair project. I love cuttlefish. I had read that they were intelligent. I had wanted to find ways to talk to them. Cuttlefish, however, do not like to be petted, nor do they enjoy chocolate cake.

"In contrast to Erma's fourth grade science fair project . . ." The headmaster continued talking, and I continued thinking. I was little when it happened, but even I remembered Erma's fourth grade science fair project. Erma had made progress towards the discovery of cold fusion. She won first place in the science fair, got her picture taken for the local newspaper, and became a runner-up for an international science achievement award.

"But, but—" Mom tried to think of more to say. Dad gently laid a hand on her shoulder. She fell silent.

"I am afraid I have no choice. Nicholas cannot attend the Institution for Children of Superior Intellectual Merit," the headmaster concluded.

I thought that meant we could go soon. Unfortunately, it did not. My parents and the headmaster kept talking. They talked about where I should go to school instead. They talked about my potential strengths (if I had any). They talked about how I could avoid being a burden to society. In short, they talked about boring things. Sometimes geniuses talk too much about boring things.

I swung my legs back and forth. I began to thumb wrestle with myself, imagining that my thumbs were opposing long-necked dinosaurs. I glanced at the clock. I wanted to go home. Something important was waiting for me in the attic.

Finally I heard Dad say, "Thank you for your time, sir."

"I wish Nicholas the best." The headmaster shook Dad's hand and smiled at me.

Soon my parents and I were back outside in the hot summer air. Jude, our butler, was waiting for us in the car. He held his pocket watch in hand. He was always on schedule—just like a clock.

Jude helped Dad get into the front passenger seat. Jude isn't a genius, but he can fold Dad's wheelchair and pack it in the trunk faster than anyone. Mom and I sat in the back seats. The car began moving. I was thankful for the breeze. I took off my hat and coat.

No one spoke of the meeting with the headmaster. Jude did not ask. I watched the scenery go by. People played in the park. A man walked his dog. A lady painted trees on a big canvas. None of them seemed to care that I wasn't a genius. The drive home seemed longer than usual.

"So how'd it go?" Erma asked once we arrived.

I cringed. Why couldn't Erma be a little more like Jude? Why did she have to ask so many questions all the time?

"Nick will not be attending the Institution for Children of Superior Intellectual Merit," Dad said.

Erma smirked. Her lip curled upward like a snake.

"But we still love Nick," Mom said fiercely.

Erma's snake-like smile vanished.

"Too bad," she said. Was she referring to the results of the meeting or the fact that Mom still loved me? She turned away and headed to her room.

"I'm sorry to hear the news, Nick," Calla said. Calla is our family's nanny. She also helps Mom in the science lab. I hadn't noticed her come in. Calla held baby Addie in her arms. Addie began to blow spit bubbles with her mouth. The bubbles grew and popped, spraying saliva into the air. Addie giggled. I think that meant Addie still loved me too.

"It's okay," I said.

"Of course it is," Dad said. "You'll just go to a different school than Erma. That's all."

Addie stopped blowing spit bubbles and began babbling.

"There's an excellent school not too far from home," Mom said. "I've heard that it's one of the best for, umm, children of average intellectual merit."

"I'll be in the attic," I said. On the way there, I met Edison, our dog. He bounded up to me on his wide paws. His nails clicked against the wooden floor. He licked my hand with his wet tongue. He wagged his tail. "Hey, buddy," I said. I patted his furry head.

I heard a loud "meow." Tesla, our black cat, sat high up on the shelf that displayed Erma's many trophies. He hid in their tall shadows. Tesla balanced carefully on his perch. He never knocked anything over, but I wouldn't mind if he knocked a trophy down just once.

I crawled inside the attic. The smell of mothballs greeted me. Erma says mothballs stink, but I like the smell. It reminds me of Grandfather, although I've never met him.

I clicked the light bulb on. The only other light came from a small window. An old dress form stood against the wall. Next to it sat a battered trunk covered with stickers. The stickers displayed names of places Grandfather had visited. He had traveled to many countries beyond Thauma. He had even visited Oreshaffe, our nation's opponent after the war. I looked beyond the trunk and saw more boxes—a heap of unexplored treasure.

I went up to the old trunk. On top sat a smaller box. I had found it just that morning. I opened it and smiled. The thing inside was beautiful. It was genius.

Well, it had been. Now it was broken. I took out an object. A metal feather. Etched into it in fine letters was the name, "Nicholas Newton." That's my grandfather. I was named after him. You might have heard about him. He's the general who ended the Last War. And, yes, he was also a genius. Now I have one of his inventions. I might not be a genius, but I'm going to fix it.

2 THE ART OF SCIENCE

The next day I began repairing Grandfather's invention. I borrowed tools from Mom's science lab. I borrowed tools from Dad's art studio. Of course, I asked first.

Because I'm not a genius, I always follow the instructions when I put something together. I didn't exactly have instructions for Grandfather's broken invention, but I did find a notebook of drawings. It came in the box. Grandfather must have drawn the pictures in the notebook. His name was written on the cover. Inside he showed how the parts fit together. How hard could it be?

I turned to the last page. The final drawing showed a clockwork bird. I carried the box and the notebook downstairs into the living room.

We have a little table in our living room. When guests come over, they set their books and coffee mugs on it.

Then they talk about genius things. Dr. Cedric sometimes brings his jar of leeches. He loves leeches as much as I love cuttlefish.

Today the table was empty. I set my box down. A gigantic portrait of Grandfather hung on the wall behind the table. Encased in a fancy golden frame, Grandfather wore his military coat covered with medals.

I sat on the floor, unpacked the box, and started working. I liked feeling the weight of the tools in my hands. I liked touching the smooth metal pieces. I liked the smell of Grandfather's notebook. The smell of old paper tickles my nose.

One of the pieces was shaped like a ball. A thin seam ran around the middle. I tried to pull it apart. It wouldn't open. I set it aside. I would follow the instructions and use it when I was told to.

I worked all day putting the invention together. I followed Grandfather's instructions exactly. The feathers clicked into various slots. I screwed the beak into what looked like the head. I balanced the metal ball on top. That was the last piece. The invention was complete!

But what was I supposed to do with all these extra pieces? Sometimes grown-ups don't make sense, even if they're geniuses.

I stood back from the table. I looked up at the portrait of Grandfather. He would be so proud. I had found his invention, and I had made it like new again.

I looked down at the finished project. Uh-oh. I looked at the picture in Grandfather's notebook. Something wasn't right. I looked at the invention again. Something was really not right.

I heard the familiar creak of Dad's wheelchair against the floor. He came into the living room. He smiled.

"Did you make that, son?" Dad always calls me "son" when he's proud of me. This time, however, I did not know why. Like I said, sometimes grown-ups don't make sense, even if they're geniuses.

"Why, son, this is brilliant!" Dad wheeled himself closer. I hid my face with the notebook. I stared at the picture Grandfather had drawn. I didn't want to see the mess I had made. Dad continued his praise. I couldn't understand him.

"The way that the lines of the sculpture meet at these angles," Dad said, "does a superb job of showing how nature, though elegant, also decays. This sphere balanced against these supports shows how people impact each other through their actions. Every person has an impact on another life."

"Dad," I said.

Dad wasn't listening. He continued babbling. He sounded a bit like baby Addie. Actually, I think Addie might have made more sense. "And the placement of this gear shows the dangers of bad choices and their unintended consequences. Our choices, in tandem with our associations—"

"Dad!"

Dad kept on going. He was talking at full speed. Sometimes he talks like this when he gives lectures at the art museum. I don't understand those either, but at least we get free cake afterwards. Then Dad's speech ended, and he asked, "Is this truly your own design?"

"Dad, it needs to look like this!" I turned the notebook around. I showed him Grandfather's picture. Grandfather's picture looked nothing like the thing I had put together.

"Oh," Dad said, staring at the drawing. He moved his glasses higher on his nose. "I see. Well, that works too." Dad wheeled out of the room and went back into his studio.

I began taking the invention apart. I put the pieces and the book back into the box. I would try again tomorrow.

3 HEADS UP!

I once again brought my tools, Grandfather's notebook, and box of parts down to the living room. I once again unpacked the box and opened the book. I took a deep breath. *I can do this*, I thought to myself. I picked up a screwdriver and began to work.

I made it to page five of Grandfather's instructions. This time a bird was starting to take shape. I could tell the head from the tail. It had a body. Maybe it wasn't fine art, but it was good. It was what Grandfather had wanted.

In the afternoon I took a break for lunch. Then I began to put the wings together. Thin sheets of metal formed the largest feathers, including the feather stamped with Grandfather's name. I carefully slid each feather into place. All was going well.

Then I heard the familiar *goo* and *ba* of baby Addie. But Addie usually crawls on the ground. Her sounds are supposed to come from below. This time they sounded like they were coming from above. Addie had either suddenly grown taller, or she had learned to fly.

As it turned out, the latter was true.

"Heads up!" Mom yelled. I looked up. Addie zoomed through the air. She was strapped into a jet pack.

Mom ran into the living room. Calla dashed right behind. For a moment the three of us watched Addie soar above our heads, babbling happily.

But as the cliché says, what goes up must come down. Those could be words to live by, especially if you take up skydiving. But I did not recall them until after it was too late.

Addie swooped low over the table—the same table where I had been working all day. Bam! Parts flew everywhere!

Addie began to cry. I stared at the pieces all over the floor. I felt like crying too.

Thankfully, Addie wasn't hurt. Mom caught her and tried to calm her down.

Even so, Mom was excited. "It's okay, Addie," she cooed. She bounced Addie in her arms. Then she grinned. "Did you see that? She was really flying. She flew!"

Dad quickly wheeled himself out of his art studio and into the living room. "What's going on in here?" he asked. "Is everyone OK?"

"I don't think Dr. Newton's jet pack baby carrier is ready yet," Calla said in her usual soft voice. Whenever she talks, it sounds like she's speaking into a blanket.

"It worked," Mom said. "Addie was flying!" Mom unstrapped Addie's jet pack. She hugged her. Addie began to laugh and giggle.

I took a closer look at the jet pack. It seemed like a normal baby carrier, but it had two big rockets on the back.

"Now I know that there's a problem with the controls," Mom said. "Addie pressed a button by accident. I need to prevent that. Maybe if I move the button more towards the side . . ."

"That sounds like a good idea, Carbon." Carbon is Dad's pet name for Mom. Some moms and dads call each other "Honey," but Dad calls Mom "Carbon." Carbon is a very important substance. We wouldn't be alive without it. Dad says that we can live without honey, but we can't live without carbon. That's why he calls her Carbon.

"I'll make the jet pack better," Mom said. "One day I'll even make your wheelchair fly!"

Dad clutched the wheels on either side of his chair. "Oh, Carbon, I like my chair the way it is, thank you." Dad laughed nervously.

"Wouldn't it be nice if our whole family could fly? Birds don't know how good they've got it," Mom said.

Dad wheeled back into his studio. Mom followed. She kept talking about flying.

Calla turned to me. "Do you need any help, Nick?" She surveyed the messy room. "You know how our butler Jude is. He doesn't like clutter."

I know very well how Jude is. Sometimes he can be rather scary when it comes to disorder. "No, thanks, I'll be OK," I said.

Calla left. I searched all over the room collecting the scattered parts. I would try again tomorrow.

AGAIN 4

The next day I worked in my bedroom instead of the living room. I set the box on my desk. I opened Grandfather's notebook. For the third time, I got to work. Today I would finish this project.

I heard a knock on my door. "Nick, did you take my book on differential calculus?" It was Erma. Differential calculus is like addition, but harder.

I opened the door. Erma had her arms folded across her chest. She frowned.

"Why would I take your book on differential calculus?" I asked. "Fourth grade math was hard enough."

"I don't know why you took it," Erma said. "I just know it's gone."

"Well, I don't have it. I didn't take it."

Erma stared past my shoulder and into my room. "What are you doing?"

"Nothing," I said. I didn't want Erma's help. She may be a genius, but I didn't want to work with a genius like her.

"That doesn't look like *nothing*." Erma craned her neck to get a better look. "Let me see."

"Why don't you go search for your calculus book?"

Erma pushed herself past me and into my room. She began touching all the pieces on my desk. She flipped through Grandfather's notebook.

"Hey, quit it."

"Do Mom and Dad know about this?" Erma continued to touch everything.

"They saw it earlier."

"You'd better be careful. It could be dangerous. Grandfather made weapons during the Last War, you know."

"It's a bird," I said. "It's not dangerous."

"Do you know what it does?"

"I don't know. It flies, I guess. It has wings."

Erma laughed. Even her laughter sounded smarter than mine. "Weapons can fly too."

"Grandfather made lots of things. He didn't just make weapons."

"Oh yeah? What else did he make?"

I thought about some of the books I had read. They had been filled with facts about Grandfather and the Last War. He had invented guns and cannons. He had modified flying machines, boats, and trains to carry them.

"Grandfather made all sorts of things," I said. "Such as, such as . . ."

Erma smiled smugly.

I heard another knock at the door. This time it was our butler Jude. Jude always knocks, even if the door is open. He held a large, thick book in his hand.

"Is this yours, Erma?" Jude held out the book. The words *Differential Calculus* were stamped on the front. "I found it on the kitchen table."

"Thank you, Jude." Erma walked to the door and took the book. She shot a glance back at me. "I'd be careful if I were you." She walked away.

"Hey, Jude," I said before he could leave. "You knew Grandfather. Did he ever make anything other than weapons?"

"Of course," Jude said. "Your Grandfather made many things."

I ran over to my desk and picked up Grandfather's notebook. "Do you know what this is? It looks like a bird. Is it anything else?" I turned to the last picture and showed it to Jude.

"Interesting. However, I have never seen it before. I am sorry I can't help you." He stared at the notebook. "Where did you find this?"

"In the attic. You can look through the notebook if you'd like."

Jude took the notebook from my hands. He handled it like Mom handles rare scientific specimens. I watched him look through the pages in silence.

Well, almost silence. I heard a soft tick-tock sound. I wondered where it came from. I didn't see Jude's pocket watch. Usually he wore the watch chain draped against the front of his vest, the watch tucked into a pocket.

"Jude, where is your pocket watch?"

"I don't need it at the moment. It is in my room."

"Then what's that ticking sound?"

Jude returned the notebook. "From one of your Grandfather's inventions," he said. "One that is most certainly not a weapon." Jude rarely smiles, but he smiled then. I watched him walk away. I now had more questions than ever. First I wondered about the bird. Now I wondered about Jude.

Perhaps putting the bird together would lead me to clues. Maybe it could answer some of my questions. But first I had to finish it.

I kept working. I made progress, but I found that some of the pieces had been broken from yesterday's encounter with the flying baby. I began searching for tape and glue. I looked high and low. Glue sticks do not work well on metal. Neither does chewing gum. I would try again tomorrow.

5 ENOUGH SAID

Always, always,

ALWAYS

ask your mother

before borrowing her
welding torch.

6 HELP WANTED

Mom was pretty upset about the welding torch. She punished me by giving me no dessert for a week. I told her I was sorry. I said I would never do it again. And I meant it. I love chocolate cake.

The next day I asked Dad for help. Maybe he could glue the broken pieces back together. I went into his art studio. I held out the broken pieces. "Can you fix them?" I asked.

"Probably," he said.

Dad looked through a drawer labeled *glue*. He had hot glue guns, glue tubes, and glue bottles arranged by type, size, and brand. He took out a fat grey tube. He wheeled over to his desk.

"Here, let me do it." Dad held out his hand. "This glue can make your fingers stick together for a long time. You need to be careful."

I wanted to put the bird together by myself, but I couldn't do it if my fingers were stuck together. I handed the broken pieces to Dad. "It's supposed to look like this." I showed Dad the picture in Grandfather's notebook.

"You know," Dad said, "this little bird is a work of art in its own right, isn't it?"

He squinted at the picture in the notebook and set up the broken pieces on his desk. Then he opened the tube of glue and squeezed a few drops onto one of the broken edges.

I glanced at the wall, which displayed two of Dad's newest paintings. One painting was black and white. It showed a deer walking through the snow.

The other picture didn't look like anything. It was a bunch of squiggly pink blobs against a red background. Strands of grey and silver streaked through it. Erma didn't like it. She said it looked like bacteria. Whatever it was, the geniuses at the art museum sure liked it. They gave it an award. Next week they were taking it away for an exhibit at the museum. But they weren't interested in the painting of the deer.

"Dad, do you think this bird is dangerous?"

"It doesn't look dangerous. Why do you ask?"

"Erma said Grandfather made weapons. What if the bird is a weapon too?"

"I don't think the bird is a weapon. Besides, Grandfather only made weapons during the war. He did other things once the war was over."

"Like what?"

"He loved robots. This bird may have been one of his first. It looks rather simple. The later ones were more complex."

I suddenly thought of Jude. I thought of the mysterious tick-tock sound—the sound that hadn't been from his pocket watch.

"Dad, may I have a new eraser?" Erma stood at the door. She held up a tiny pink nub, all that was left of her old eraser.

"Third drawer on the right," Dad said. He didn't even need to look up. Dad knew his studio like that deer knew its forest.

Erma walked to the drawer, pulled it open, and found a fat eraser. This time she chose a blue one. Erma came up to the desk.

"Dad," Erma moaned, "why are you helping him with that? Nobody even knows what it does."

"Don't worry about it," Dad said. "It can't be any more dangerous than Mom's flying baby jet packs."

Erma looked at the bird. "It may not be dangerous, but it's still a waste of time."

"Now, Erma, you don't know that," Dad said. "Grandfather's inventions are very valuable."

"I don't think that fixing a little bird is going to win a prize at the Grand Fair. The project I'm working on is sure to win."

"Maybe I don't want a prize," I said.

"Of course you'd say that. You'll never get a prize. You're not a genius."

"Erma," Dad scolded. "Prizes are never to be valued over people. You will not talk to your brother that way."

"Sorry." Erma sulked out of the room. Her fist clenched around the eraser.

Dad shook his head. "I'm not entering the Grand Fair."

"You're not? Why?"

"I'm busy with too many projects as it is. And besides, I'd like to see another artist win this year. When I enter a contest, I always come home with a prize. I'm sure a prize from the Grand Fair would mean more to someone else."

This would be the first time Dad didn't submit art to the Grand Fair. Ever since I could remember, the Fair has been one of the highlights of the year. People come from all across the country of Thauma. I've noticed people from Oreshaffe too. The scientists show off their newest inventions and talk about their latest discoveries. The artists get together to display and perform their best work. Even though I never get to participate, I like watching.

"All done." Dad put the cap back onto the glue tube. I looked at the fixed pieces up close. "Leave them here for now," Dad said. "The glue dries fast, but it's always safer to wait overnight. You don't want them to break again."

"Thanks, Dad."

I left the drying pieces on Dad's desk, but I took the box and Grandfather's notebook back to my room. I would continue on tomorrow.

TECHNICAL DIFFICULTIES 7

The next morning I got the glued pieces from Dad's studio and brought them into my room. I opened Grandfather's notebook and eagerly searched for the next step.

It only took a moment to find, but when I saw it, I frowned. I felt like it would take a lifetime to figure out. I didn't have a lifetime to figure it out. School started soon, and I would be busy with homework.

I grabbed a few pieces that looked like they might work. One of them was the strange metal ball. It was unlike any other piece. I studied the drawings in the notebook again. I tried putting the pieces together. They wouldn't fit.

I worked for a long time, but I was puzzled. I decided to ask Mom for help. I carried the notebook and box to Mom's science lab. I knocked on the door.

"Come in," Mom said.

I opened the door. Addie floated near the ceiling in her baby walker. She looked like a tiny alien piloting a flying saucer. But she wasn't the pilot. Mom held the control firmly in hand. She used a single knob to navigate.

When Mom saw me, she landed the saucer. Wheels came out of the bottom, and it rolled onto the floor. Addie's chubby legs touched the ground. Our nanny Calla called to Addie to come to her.

"Sorry about the welding torch," I said. I had said it before, but I wanted to let Mom know that I was really sorry—because I was.

"You don't need to keep saying that," Mom said. She smiled.

I held up the box of parts. "Can you help me with this?"

Mom looked at Calla. She was playing with a giggling Addie. Addie held a plush mouse.

"Now seems like a good time," Mom said. She sat down at her worktable. I laid out the pieces. I then showed her Grandfather's notebook. Mom opened it and studied the pages. I pointed to the confusing picture. Mom looked at it for a long time.

My eyes wandered around Mom's lab. It didn't look like Dad's art studio. Mom stored stuff in big plastic bins with no labels. The bins were scattered on top of shelves and all over the floor. The shelves were crammed with books, bottles, and tools. A preserved frog stared out of a glass jar. A telescope lens looked down from the top of a cabinet.

My eyes came back to Mom's desk. It was piled high with papers. But even though Mom's lab looked disorderly, she knew exactly where things were.

Mom tinkered with the parts. "Grandfather Newton was a very clear thinker. None of my diagrams look as neat as his."

"It still looks confusing to me," I said.

"Just because someone thinks clearly doesn't mean he's easy to understand. Nick, where did you find this old invention?" Mom held the parts I had put together earlier. She was trying to fit the metal ball into the bird's body.

"I got it from the attic."

"Hmm."

"There's a lot of stuff up there—old clothes, books, boxes."

Addie giggled behind us.

"Are you going to take the flying saucer to the fair?"

"Yes, and I have other things planned too." Mom smiled. The pieces of the bird were coming together. I watched her work.

"Mom," I asked, "is Jude a robot?"

Mom nearly dropped her screwdriver. She made a face like she was trying to hold back a sneeze. Then she began to laugh. Mom does not have a very ladylike laugh, but I like it. "What ever gave you that idea, Nick? Of course he's not a robot."

"But didn't Grandfather make robots?"

"Well, yes," Mom said, "but our butler Jude is not one of them."

Addie began to cry. She banged on the baby walker. She hit it harder and harder. Whoosh! The walker and the baby shot up into the air. Addie cried even louder. Mom leapt up from her chair. She grabbed the remote and tried to steer Addie back onto the ground.

"The control isn't working!" Mom shouted. "Nick, get out of the way!"

I quickly (but carefully) placed the bird parts back into my box and dashed towards the door. Almost there. I heard a thud and the screech of metal.

"Oh, thank goodness you're safe," I heard Mom say.

I turned. Addie was still crying, but she had landed safely. Mom took her out of the saucer, which now had a large dent on the front.

"Nick, maybe this isn't such a good time, after all," Mom said. "Maybe tomorrow, OK?"

"OK."

I went to my room. I laid out the remaining parts on my desk. I opened Grandfather's notebook. Mom had put a lot together, but the invention wasn't complete. I continued the work.

By the end of the day, I had come a long way. The invention in my hands looked very much like Grandfather's drawing. I was almost done.

FLIGHT 8

Some days Dad doesn't paint pictures or practice music. He goes out of the house. He doesn't go out to buy anything. He doesn't go out to get lunch or meet with friends or watch a play. He goes for what he calls *inspiration*. Sometimes he goes to the lake behind the house. Sometimes he goes to his favorite cafe in town. Every once in a while he goes to the museum. I like the museum too, but I don't go with him when he's searching for inspiration. Usually Dad brings Jude though.

I was almost done with Grandfather's clockwork bird. For the last step, I needed to attach the wings to the body. Then I had to wind it up with the key which was also in the box. I hoped the bird would work.

But I didn't want to put the final pieces together in my room. I wanted to go back up to the attic. I'm not sure why. I suppose I wanted some inspiration too.

I climbed the ladder. I held the box tightly to my side with one arm. I thought about Erma's words. Was the bird a weapon? *Well*, I thought, *if it explodes up here, hopefully no one else will get hurt*.

Today plenty of sunshine smiled through the attic window, and the single light bulb was as bright as ever. I laid the box on top of the trunk covered with stickers, the same spot where I had first found it.

I opened the box. I took out the bird's body. It was heavy in my hands. When I lifted it, the head swiveled sideways. It looked dead.

I took out the left wing next. I clicked it into place. The bird didn't move.

I took out the right wing. I clicked it into the other slot on the side of the bird.

The bird's head turned. The shutters that formed its eyelids lifted. It flapped its wings. It stared at me. I stared back. Then its eyes closed, and its head flopped to the side again. I scrambled for the key, placed it into the hole between the wings, and turned it several times.

The bird sprang to life. It began to sing. It sounded like a music box—a plinking sort of sound. I laughed. The bird sang a tune. It was the same song over and over, but I didn't mind. I had fixed Grandfather's invention.

The bird flapped its wings faster and faster. It lifted itself out of my hands. It hovered and wobbled in front of my face. I reached out my hand and tried to touch it. It flew forward, but instead of perching nicely on my hand, it pecked me on top of the head.

"Ouch!" It pecked my head over and over. "Ow! Ow! Ow!"

I imagined Erma nagging at me. "I told you so," she would say. "That bird is a weapon."

I rubbed my head. The bird flew off and bumped into a stack of boxes. It flew higher until it hit the ceiling. Then it almost got stuck in the bell of a phonograph.

I tried to catch it. "Come back. Please don't run away."

The bird crashed into the dress form. Its pointed beak left a hole in the fabric. Then it zoomed down the ladder faster than I could climb.

I darted towards Dad's studio, the bird still ahead of me. My feet must have made a lot of noise. Dad poked his head out of the studio. "What's the rush, Nick?"

"It's flying away!" I ran to keep up. The bird wasn't bumping into things as much anymore.

Mom was testing the flying saucer in the living room. This time the saucer had a padded bumper wrapped around the edge.

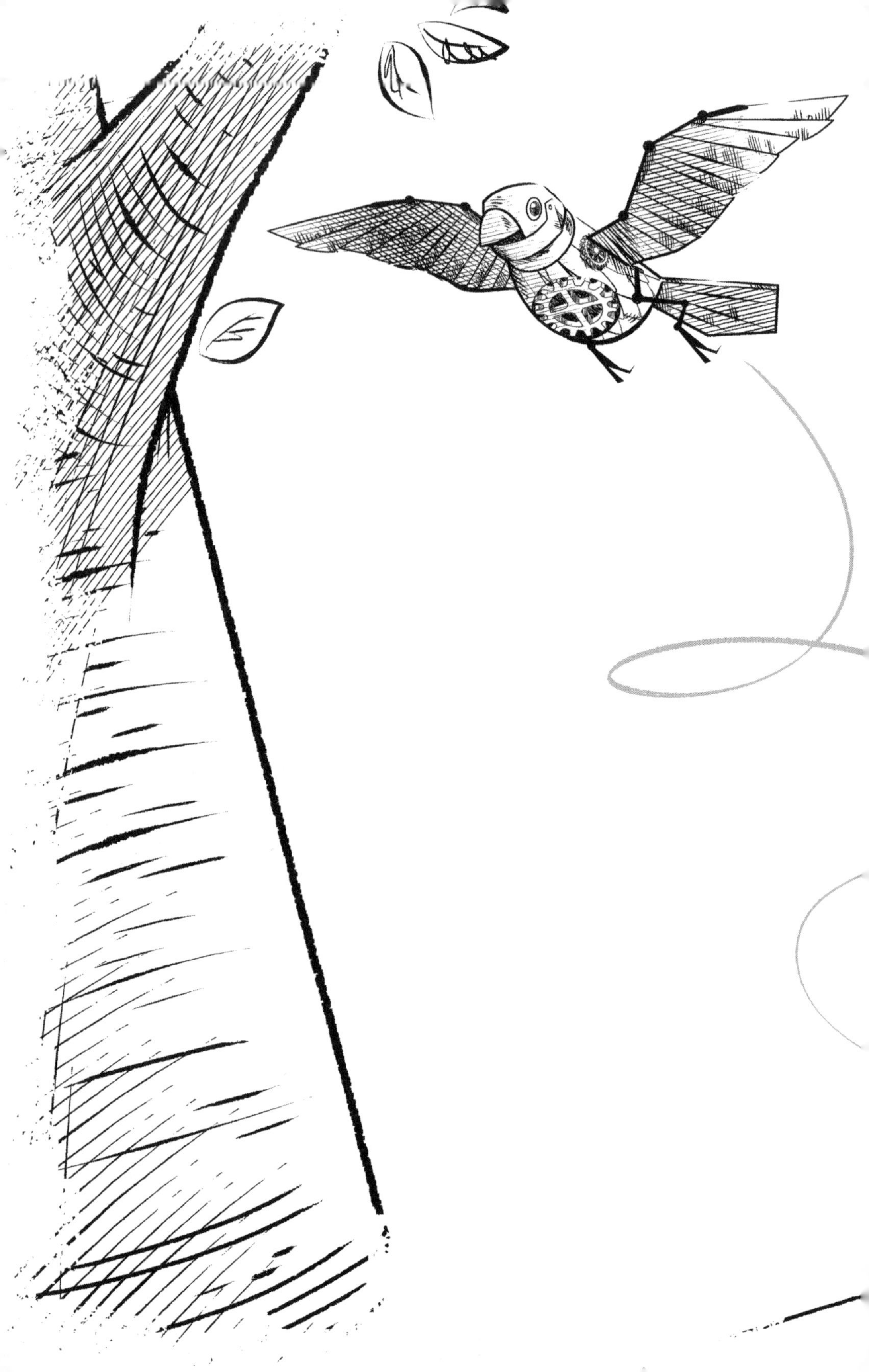

Mom was quick to notice the bird. “It looks wonderful, Nick.”

“But it’s getting away.”

I’m not sure if Addie knew what was happening, but her baby babble sounded more urgent than usual. “Goo!” she shouted.

“That’s right, Addie,” Mom said.

I don’t think Mom understood Addie either, but soon Addie’s flying saucer was speeding after the bird. Mom held the control with both hands. Addie squealed with delight. She began to flap her arms like wings.

The bird was closing in on the door.

“It’s going to crash!” I shouted.

The door flew open just in time. Erma stood on the other side. She held a bucket of paint in her hand. She screamed. Paint flew everywhere.

The bird zoomed out the door. My feet tracked through the paint. Colorful footprints trailed behind me as I continued the chase.

Tesla was sitting on the porch. Like any cat, his ears perked up at the sight of a bird, and he sprang after it. His feet got into the paint. Colorful paw prints trailed behind him.

“We’re not letting it get away,” Mom said.

“Ba-ba-ba,” Addie agreed.

Mom maneuvered the flying saucer outside. We were catching up to the bird. Calla stayed behind. She helped Erma clean up the spilled paint.

I almost forgot an important rule. I'm not allowed to go out of the yard by myself. Thankfully the bird turned at the last moment and flew behind the house.

There's a big tree in our back yard. The bird flew right into the branches. It didn't come down. It started to screech.

The screech sounded worse than the time I tried to play the violin. Addie started to cry. I covered my ears. The clockwork bird was stuck in the tree.

9 TO THE RESCUE

"Make it stop!" Erma shouted.

Erma and Calla stood next to me. I looked up into the tree. I could barely see the bird through the branches. Mom landed the flying saucer. She took Addie out. "Calla, please take Addie inside."

Calla took Addie into her arms. They went inside.

"Erma, please let me know before you paint the porch." Dad had joined us. Jude stood behind him. "I like the design," Dad said, "but that paint will rub off in a few days. Next time we'll buy outdoor paint. Now, what's making that horrible noise?"

Erma pointed up. The bird wouldn't stop screeching, and the tree was too big to climb.

"I have an idea," I said. Everyone looked at me. I am not a genius. I don't usually have good ideas. "I'll sit in the flying saucer, fly up, and rescue the bird."

"Let's try that," Mom said.

"That's the spirit," Dad said.

"It won't work," Erma said.

I threw off my coat and hat. I sat down on the saucer. I was barely small enough to fit. I felt funny sitting in a baby walker, but I had a job to do.

Mom handed me the controls. "You can fly the saucer yourself. It'll be easier for you to get through the branches."

I pressed the button, launching the saucer into the air. It wobbled. "Whoa," I said. The saucer began floating gently. That was much better.

I flew higher. The ground shrank. Flying was fun.

Whack! Bumping into branches was not fun.

I bumped into a lot of branches, but I finally came to the bird. Its screeching was louder than ever, but I couldn't cover my ears. I needed both hands to steer the saucer and catch the bird.

I reached out to the bird. It stopped screeching. I smiled. Maybe the bird would be my friend if I saved it. It snapped at my fingers. Then again, maybe not.

"I'm trying to help you," I said.

The bird did not seem to care.

I tried talking louder and more slowly. "I'm . . . trying . . . to . . . help . . . you."

"That won't work," Erma shouted from below.

The bird began to peck the tree. Now that it was distracted, I grabbed its smooth metal body. I pulled it off the branch. I brought it in close.

Straining its neck, it pecked the saucer's control switch. "Uh-oh."

I began to fall. The bird had turned the saucer off!

I hit more branches on the way down. Maybe putting the bird together had been a bad idea.

"I'll catch you," Jude said.

Thud!

I kind of wished Jude was fatter. Then he would have given me more cushioning when I fell. Even so, I was alive, and the bird was out of the tree.

"My saucer!" Mom ran over and grabbed her saucer out of the pile. "It still needs a lot of work."

"Hey, where's the bird?" I sat up and dusted myself off.

The bird swooped down and pecked my head.

Jude stood and looked at the bird. "Stop that right now."

The bird paused, landed on the ground, and began to sing.

"Wow." Erma got closer. She tried to touch the bird. It snapped at her fingers. "The bird listens to Jude, but it doesn't like anyone else."

Jude held out his hand. The bird perched on his finger.

"You can keep it," I said. "It seems happy with you. I want it to be happy."

"Well, bird," Jude said. "Hmm . . . you need a name. I'm afraid I'm not good with names."

The bird sang its song again.

"Plink," I said. "Its name—her name—is Plink."

"Well, Plink," Jude said, "you should listen to Nick. You will stop pecking him, and you will live with him from now on."

Jude presented the bird to me. She perched on my finger. She did not peck.

Mom set down the broken saucer and watched Plink. “It looks like your problem is solved, Nick.”

“It looks like it.” I smiled, and Plink chirped another tune.

Part Two

10 LESSONS FROM JUDE

The school year was starting soon. Erma knew exactly where she was going to school. She was going to the Institution for Children of Superior Intellectual Merit. I, however, am not a child of superior intellectual merit. I thought I was going back to my old school, but Mom had other ideas.

"I don't think Nick's current school gives him enough opportunities," Mom said.

"What do you mean, Carbon?" Dad asked.

"Nick should go to a school that fosters his unique talents and abilities."

Mom and Dad took me to visit a lot of schools. One was a magnet school. I thought I would learn about magnets, but instead I learned about math. I'm not good at math. We visited a year-round school. I didn't want to go to school throughout the whole year. "Erma gets a long summer break," I said. "Can't I get one too?"

"If Nick goes to school year-round," Mom said, "it might be harder to plan for vacations."

"Perhaps we should try something else," Dad said.

"But we're running out of time," Mom said. "School starts soon, and we can't let Nick fall behind."

"Don't worry, Carbon."

Erma's school started tomorrow. "We should've looked for schools earlier," Mom said.

"We'll figure something out."

The something was that Jude would tutor me until we found a school. I wasn't expecting this. Neither was Jude.

"Today we will be learning about the political system of our most excellent country of Thauma," Jude said.

I sat on the living room couch with a notebook and pen in my hands. A chalkboard on wheels had been set up opposite the couch. Jude began scribbling notes on the chalkboard. His handwriting was very neat. Everything Jude does is precise.

Plink sat on top of my head. She chirped. Jude turned around and gave her a disapproving glance. "Nick, what can you tell me about the Senate?"

"What?" I had no interest in politics.

"The Senate is very important." Jude began writing on the chalkboard again. "Senators are responsible for . . ."

I raised my hand. "Umm, Jude?"

"Yes, Nick?" He turned around.

"When are we going to learn about the Last War?"

"What?"

"You know, the Last War, when Thauma fought against Oreshaffe. I would like to learn more about what Grandfather did."

"We'll get to that another day." Jude droned on and on about the Senate. I had never heard him talk so much before, and I had no idea that he knew so much about politics. I wish he had known as much about the Last War.

Lessons finally ended. Jude had to go get Erma from the Institution for Children of Superior Intellectual Merit. I was glad. I had learned enough about the Senate for one day.

11 THE COLLECTOR

Jude makes an excellent butler. He is always tidy. He is always punctual. He can drive a car. But he isn't such an excellent teacher. The next day I learned all about the prime minister. I also learned some arithmetic. I already knew how to do long division, but I didn't tell Jude because I didn't want him to start up on politics again. Jude and I were in the middle of our long division when Dad wheeled into the room.

"You can stop now, Jude," Dad said. "Nick, Mom and I think we've found a good school for you. It's farther away than the magnet school, but we think you'll like it."

"Do I have to take a lot of math classes?" I asked.

"Only one class at a time," Dad said.

Jude began erasing the math on the chalkboard.

"I appreciate your efforts, Jude." Dad wheeled closer. "Thank you."

The next day I visited the new school with Mom and Dad. It was called the Volk Institute. The main building was large and white with tall glass windows.

"Oh, hello!" A young man greeted us when we walked in. He looked like he could've been in high school. He bowed dramatically, taking off his top hat with a flourish. "My, my, I never imagined that the Newtons would be interested in this humble educational facility."

As odd as he was, I wasn't paying much attention to him. I was much more interested in the robot standing behind him. I had recently learned that robots that looked like people were called androids. This one looked to be about Erma's age. Plink, who had been sitting silently on my shoulder, flew over to get a closer look.

Mom smiled at the young man. "We're looking for a school for our son, Nick. Are you a student here?"

"Ha-ha-ha. No. I actually graduated some time ago."

"Oh, I'm sorry. My mistake."

"It's quite all right. I get that all the time. I am Solomon Volk."

"*The* Solomon Volk?" Dad said, surprised. "The one whose family built this school?"

"Yes," Mr. Volk said. "Sometimes I visit to see how things are going. At the moment I think the school could use a bigger building for the arts—a better performance hall perhaps."

"That sounds splendid," Dad said.

"Would you like me to show you around?" Mr. Volk asked.

"Lead the way."

My parents chatted with Mr. Volk, but I followed without saying a word. I was too fascinated by the android. The android did not speak, but her glass eyes looked arrogantly at the world as if everything in it were beneath her. She wore a dress that matched Mr. Volk's white suit. If she hadn't been moving, I would have mistaken her for a life-size china doll.

Mr. Volk led us into a hallway of classrooms. "Your son will probably be learning in one of these rooms. You said he was entering fifth grade. Correct?" He led us away from the hall and into another building.

"This is the gymnasium," Mr. Volk said. It was a large, open building that looked a lot like the gym in my old school.

"Mr. Volk, are you a genius?"

"Nick!" both Mom and Dad said at once.

"Please excuse our son." Dad frowned at me, but Mr. Volk laughed.

"A valid question." He shook his head. "No, I am not a genius. In fact, I'll let you in on a little secret." His voice grew softer, but there was no one else around to hear. "My parents started this school for me. After they found out I *wasn't* a genius, they were still determined to send me to an excellent school. So they built one. They funded the construction of the buildings. They hired the finest teachers. They bought books. Other students came too, if they could afford it."

Mr. Volk was interrupted by a loud crash. He whirled around. "Elizabeth!" he shouted.

A pink rubber ball rolled out from behind a door. The android followed, holding a purple ball with both hands. Plink flew over and perched on the android's head.

"I'm terribly sorry," Mr. Volk said. "I should've known that Elizabeth would want to play if we came into the gym."

More balls rolled out from behind the door.

"Put the balls back, Elizabeth."

Elizabeth lowered her head as if saddened, but she obediently began rolling the balls back to where they belonged. Plink nudged the balls with her beak. After all of the balls were returned, Elizabeth stood beside Mr. Volk, and Plink returned to me.

"Don't mind Elizabeth. She has a few quirks in her programming."

Plink chirped and looked at Elizabeth.

"And what a fine specimen you have here." Mr. Volk took a closer look at Plink. "An exquisite creation. So small and yet so detailed."

"This is Plink," I said, feeling proud. I took her off my shoulder and held her up.

"My grandfather made her, but I found her and put her back together again."

"An original by General Newton? A rare find." Mr. Volk was clearly impressed.

"It's just an old toy," Mom said. She tried to change the subject. "I'm sure your android is much more advanced. You said her name was Elizabeth? What a pretty name."

"Yes, yes, your android is certainly more sophisticated," Dad said. "This bird is one of Grandfather Newton's early models. Rather primitive, you might say."

Mr. Volk pulled out his wallet. He opened it and yanked out a fistful of bills. "How much?" he asked.

I tightened my grip on Plink's hard metal body.

"We're sorry, but the bird isn't for sale," Mom said.

"Name your price." Mr. Volk pulled more bills into his hand.

"Memories have no price, and neither does friendship," Dad said. "Plink is very valuable to us."

Mr. Volk smiled. "Everything has a price."

I hid Plink under my hat for the rest of the tour, which didn't take long.

When we arrived back home, Erma was sitting at the kitchen table working on homework.

"The Volk Institute seemed like a fine school," Mom said, "What did you think, Nick?"

Erma butted in. "The Volk Institute? As in Solomon Volk? He's weird."

"How do you know?" I asked, although for once I agreed with her. Mr. Volk was weird.

"Now, now," Mom said. "Mr. Volk might be slightly eccentric, but I'm sure he's a nice man."

I have since discovered that *eccentric* is the same as *weird*—but it's used for rich people. Solomon Volk was indeed eccentric.

"I've heard all about Mr. Volk," Erma said. "Some of my classmates' parents have met him. Some people say that he was raised by robots."

"That can't be true," I said. "Nobody could be raised by robots." I took my hat off. Plink flew out of my hair and sang a song.

"It doesn't matter if Mr. Volk was raised by robots," Mom said. "He's still a human being. A very wealthy human being."

"Wealthier than we are?" Erma asked.

Mom didn't answer. I think that meant yes.

Mom continued. "Erma, you've seen the new robotics lab at your school, right?"

Erma nodded. "Of course."

"Volk Enterprises donated it. Mr. Volk owns Volk Enterprises."

A VISIT FROM VOLK 12

Despite Mr. Volk's eccentricities, Mom and Dad sent in an application for me to attend his school. I waited for my acceptance letter.

A few days after submitting the application and a few more days of lessons with Jude, I heard a knock at the door. Jude stopped in the middle of lessons and went to answer it. I went to the window to see who it was.

Jude opened the door. "May I help you?"

Mr. Volk and Elizabeth stood on the porch. Mr. Volk held a briefcase. He tipped his hat to Jude and smiled. "Hello. My name is Solomon Volk of Volk Enterprises. I am pleased to inform the Newtons that their son has been accepted into the Volk Institute." He took a white envelope from his pocket. "May I please speak with Mr. or Dr. Newton?"

"I assure you that I am capable of delivering the message." Jude reached for the envelope, but Mr. Volk did not give it to him.

"I would like to speak to Mr. or Dr. Newton."

Before Jude could reply, Mom's voice rang out from the driveway. She must've walked through the side door without us noticing. "I've always wanted to see one of these," she said. She walked around the unusual car parked in front of our house. She bent down on her hands and knees and took a peek underneath the car. Jude and Mr. Volk stared. Elizabeth cocked her head as if perplexed.

"Is this a new model of F-2944?" Mom stood up from her inspection.

"Why, yes, it is," Mr. Volk said, walking over to the car. "It's a prototype. Have you heard of it?"

"I most certainly have," Mom said. "There was an article about it in last month's issue of the Steam Flight Science Magazine!"

Jude cocked his head, unintentionally mimicking Elizabeth's expression. Mom pointed to the car and looked at Jude. "It's a car that can fly."

"Hopefully," Mr. Volk said. "Since it's a prototype, it doesn't have its hot air balloon installed yet."

"Wouldn't it be exciting to drive a car that could fly?" Mom touched the car door fondly.

"Oh, it's only a toy. And a rather crude one at that." Mr. Volk glanced at the window where I stood. I shrank behind the curtain. Plink pressed against my neck. I felt her tiny metal claws grip into my shoulder. "It's not nearly as spectacular as your son's clockwork bird. That is a true treasure."

I don't think Mom heard what Mr. Volk had said. She was too focused on the car. "When do you think you'll have these ready for sale?" she asked.

"It still needs a lot of work, and it will take years to pass safety testing in flight mode. Even I won't be able to fly in it for quite some time."

"What's going on out here?" Dad wheeled down the hall and parked next to Jude.

"Come look at the flying car," Mom said.

Dad wheeled down the ramp.

"My company is constantly working on new projects. This flying car is only one of them," Mr. Volk said. "How would the Newtons like to go on a private tour of Volk Enterprises?"

"That sounds splendid," Mom said. She touched Dad's shoulder. "What do you think?"

"I don't see why not, Carbon," Dad said. "What time would be good for you, Mr. Volk?"

Mr. Volk took a planner from his pocket. "Hmm . . . Friday I have to run the weekly robot maintenance routine, but I have a few free hours Saturday."

As my parents and Mr. Volk discussed their schedules, Jude went back into the living room. He picked up a piece of chalk. "Nick, let's resume your lessons."

Plink flew off my shoulder and back to the couch. I reluctantly left the window. I didn't exactly like Mr. Volk, but I sure liked his car.

I sat down. Jude continued as if nothing had interrupted us. But the lesson was interrupted again when Mom and Dad came back inside.

"We're going to tour Volk Enterprises on Saturday," Mom said. "Won't that be wondrous? I wonder what else Mr. Volk is working on? A flying train perhaps?"

"That's not the only news." Dad handed me the envelope. "Congratulations. You've been accepted into the Volk Institute. You can start classes tomorrow."

"Great," I said.

"You don't sound excited," Mom said. "Are you still sad that you can't go to Erma's school? Is that it?"

"No, it's not that."

"We've talked about this a lot, Nick," Dad said. "We're proud of you whatever school you go to."

"What if Mr. Volk keeps trying to buy Plink?" I asked. "Do you think he'd steal her?"

"We won't let that happen," Jude said, and he said it like he meant it. He cleared the chalkboard and returned the books to the shelf. He glanced at his pocket watch and said, "Oh, look at the time. I need to pick Erma up from school."

13 THE NEW KID

The Volk Institute was bigger than my old school. After all, it wasn't just an elementary school. It included middle and high school too.

I tucked Plink into a pocket of my book bag. "Don't make a sound, OK?"

Plink chirped. I snapped the pocket shut.

Jude drove Erma and me to school. Erma's school was closer to our house, so she was dropped off first. Jude and I were left together for a few moments. I thought he might start talking about politics again, but he didn't say anything.

Soon the car stopped. We had arrived at the Volk Institute.

"I wish you the best, Nick."

"Thank you." I took a deep breath, walked up the stairs, and entered the building.

Finding my classroom was easy. Once there, I had planned to take a seat in the back and blend into the crowd. But the teacher, Mrs. Bonswoggle, would have none of that. No sooner had I entered the room than she exclaimed, "Here is our new student, Nicholas Newton!" She ushered me to the front of the room. "Class, remember General Newton from our exciting history lessons? This is his grandson!"

I felt my face turning red. Mrs. Bonswoggle continued. "Remember the butterflies we studied in science class? Nicholas's mother discovered one of them."

Several of my new classmates snickered. I felt my hands ooze with sweat. Just as Mrs. Bonswoggle was beginning to list my father's accomplishments, another student's voice rang out, "Hey, Nicholas, how come you're not a genius?"

"I didn't see you raise your hand, Winston," Mrs. Bonswoggle said.

Winston raised his hand, but Mrs. Bonswoggle did not call on him. She continued, "Nicholas's sister Erma attends the Institution for Children of Superior Intellectual Merit, but we are very happy to have Nick in our class. Aren't we, class?" Mrs. Bonswoggle pointed to a seat in the front row. "Please have a seat, Nicholas." I sat where I was told, and Mrs. Bonswoggle strode to her desk. "Let's begin today's lessons."

I sat right in front of Winston. He kicked the back of my seat with his long legs. By the time math class came, I had had enough.

"Could you please stop that?" I whispered, turning around.

"No talking during class, Nicholas," Mrs. Bonswoggle said.

Winston continued kicking my chair. But that wasn't the worst experience of the day. At least Plink had stayed quiet during class. Not so during PE.

I didn't want to leave Plink, so I moved her into my gym bag before anyone could notice. Mr. Harrison, the PE teacher, blew a shiny whistle to get our attention. Unfortunately, it got Plink's attention too. She had never heard a whistle before. Or rather, I had never watched her react to one. She shot out of my bag like a bullet.

"What is that?" Mr. Harrison shouted. Plink sped toward him. Mr. Harrison ducked, but not low enough. Plink grazed the top of his head.

It was already sort of obvious, but Mr. Harrison wore a toupee. Plink's tiny claws snagged the toupee and ripped it right off his head, exposing the shiny bald surface underneath. I watched in silence, stunned and embarrassed. But not as embarrassed as Mr. Harrison. I opened my mouth to apologize, but before I could get a word out, I heard laughter. At first I thought it was another student. I turned around. It was Mr. Volk.

Elizabeth stood beside him in silence. She wore her perpetually bored expression. Mr. Volk carried long rolls of paper. They looked like blueprints. Sometimes Dad drew on paper like that. Hadn't Mr. Volk mentioned adding a new building to the school? Maybe he was here to work on the building.

Mr. Harrison's face was red. I may not be a genius, but I could tell he was angry.

"N-Newton!" he barked. He pointed at me.

Plink had landed in my cupped hands. She still clutched the toupee, which surrounded her like a furry nest.

"Give that back right now!"

"Now, Mr. Harrison, there's no need to shout." Mr. Volk walked over to us. "I'm sure Ned and his little bird didn't mean any harm."

Mr. Harrison, a very large man, shrank in Mr. Volk's presence.

"Y-yes, sir," Mr. Harrison said.

"Now, Ned—"

"Nick," I said.

"Would you please return Mr. Harrison's toupee?"

Plink flew up, dropped the toupee onto Mr. Harrison's head, and flew back to me. Mr. Harrison scrambled to adjust the hairpiece.

"What a troublesome little toy," Mr. Volk said. "You know, I'd gladly take it off your hands, and I'd pay a good price."

I didn't say anything. I squeezed Plink until she chirped.

During recess, everyone wanted to see Plink. They asked questions, and I did my best to answer.

"Where'd you get it?"

"What does it do?"

"Can I hold it?"

Plink flew around our heads, just out of reach. She landed on my shoulder. I felt important.

"What's the big deal?" Winston came up to the group surrounding me. "It's just some dumb toy."

The crowd gradually dispersed. Some went to play on the swings. Others began a game of kickball. But there was one boy still standing next to me.

"I don't think your bird is a dumb toy," he said. "What's its name?"

"Her name is Plink," I said.

He smiled. "Hi, Plink." The boy reached out his finger, and Plink tried to nip it with her beak. He quickly took his hand away. "Hey, can she fight?"

"I suppose if she needed to."

Plink launched off my shoulder and did a loop in the air.

"Amazing," the boy said. "I'm Elliot." He held out his hand. "Elliot Twain."

I took his hand and suddenly regretted the decision. It was covered in slime. Elliot laughed. "Sorry. It's just glue. My glue bottle exploded after science class. I tried to keep it under control, but, you know, it's glue."

I wiped the glue off my hand and onto my pants. It left a strange orange smear, but it would wash out. I think. Plink flew over and pecked Elliot on the head.

"Ow! Cheeky little thing, aren't you?"

Plink flew back to me. She began to sing.

"She's like a music box," Elliot said.

"Say, why aren't you playing kickball with the others?"

"I like sports, but my dad doesn't let me play them. He says I'm accident-prone."

As if to prove the point, the kickball sailed through the air, made an elegant arc, and hit Elliot on the head.

"Ow!" Elliot rubbed his head. I tossed the kickball back.

"See what I mean?" Elliot began to laugh. I laughed too. Perhaps attending the Volk Institute would be fun after all.

RESEARCH AND DESIGN

"We can't be late." Mom rushed around the house, darting in and out of her laboratory. Each time she found new papers and random objects to stuff into her briefcase.

"Mom, where's my green hair ribbon?" Erma shouted.

I reached up to reposition my hat, but it was no longer on my head. I had it a moment ago. Where had it gone?

"I wonder if I should bring a gift for Mr. Volk." Dad said to no one in particular. "Yes. A splendid idea."

"Dr. Newton," Jude said, "I believe Mr. Volk would be most interested in your latest household robotics report."

Mom stopped trying to cram more paper into her briefcase. "You're right, Jude. Mr. Volk loves robots." She dumped her briefcase out and put only a single document back inside.

"Erma, your ribbon is being used as a bookmark for your literature anthology, which I found in the garden this morning." Jude handed Erma a thick book. A green ribbon stuck out from between the pages.

"Thank you, Jude." Erma took the book.

"By the way, Nick," Jude said, "I believe I saw your hat on the coffee table in the living room."

"Thanks, Jude." I went to the living room. Sure enough, the hat was on the table. Plink flew off my shoulder and retrieved it.

Finally we were ready to leave. Erma's ribbon was in her hair. My hat was on my head. Mom's briefcase contained only her most important papers. Both Calla and baby Addie were staying at home.

"Where is Mr. Newton?" Jude asked.

Dad emerged from his studio carrying a sculpture. The sculpture was an assemblage of clockwork, doll parts, and a wax banana thrown in for good measure. "I've been working on this for weeks," Dad said. "I thought that it might be nice to bring something to show our appreciation."

"I don't think that is necessary," Jude said, "but act upon what you consider proper."

Dad looked at the sculpture. He looked at Jude. He took a moment to think. "I suppose," he said, "I am rather attached to this one." Dad wheeled back into his studio to put the sculpture away.

Finally we were all in the car and heading to Volk Enterprises.

"What do you think we'll see there?" I asked.

"A lot of robots probably," Erma said. "Mr. Volk is crazy about robots. He loves them more than people."

"That's silly," I said. Plink sat on my lap. As much as I liked her, I didn't love her more than Mom or Dad.

"Mr. Volk isn't a good man," Erma said, lowering her voice. "A girl in my class said that he used robots to replace his own family."

"That is nonsense," Mom said. "Erma, we do not spread bizarre rumors about other people. Mr. Volk may be a bit . . . different . . . but he seems like a respectable person."

"Sorry," Erma said. Then she whispered in my ear, "but you never know."

It was a beautiful summer day. If we hadn't been going to such an interesting place, I would have wanted the drive to last even longer.

Jude stopped the car in front of an impressive building with a spacious lawn and huge front doors. We piled out. Plink stretched her wings. She climbed onto my head. I hid her under my hat.

I'm not sure how I had expected to be greeted. Perhaps a robot butler would come out and escort us inside. Perhaps Elizabeth would greet us. Whatever I had imagined, I wasn't prepared for what happened next.

"Intruder! Intruder! Destroy! Destroy!" A large cannon pointed straight at us. The cannon moved on its own. It looked like it was taking aim on its own too.

"What do we do?" I asked.

Erma screamed. "This was a trap!"

"Everyone, remain calm," Dad said. "I'm sure Mr. Volk has this under control."

Just when I thought the cannon would fire, Mr. Volk and Elizabeth dashed out of the building. Mr. Volk propped his foot against the back of the cannon. "Stand down, Howard."

The cannon lowered its barrel. Mr. Volk jumped aside. The cannon backed away until it had returned to its original place on the lawn. It reminded me of a dog retreating with its tail between its legs. Except, of course, the cannon didn't have a tail.

"I am terribly sorry," Mr. Volk said. "I forgot to inform Howard of your arrival. But just so you know, he's never loaded. He's actually nice when you get to know him. He's just a little overprotective, that's all."

"It's a cannon," Erma said, "not a person."

Mr. Volk looked at her like she had no idea what she was saying.

Jude walked back to the car. "I'll return at the designated time." He tugged uncomfortably at his shirt collar and wiped his brow with his handkerchief. His long legs looked shaky. Usually nothing startled Jude, not even Mom's craziest inventions or Dad's weirdest art projects.

"Sir, you are more than welcome to join us," Mr. Volk said. "You may leave the car where it is. No need to rush away."

"He's just our butler," Erma said. "You don't need to call him *sir*."

Mr. Volk frowned at her. If Mr. Volk hadn't wanted to buy Plink so badly, I might have started to like him just then.

"No, thank you," Jude said. "I am afraid I can't join. I have lots of errands to run. Yes, errands. Lots of them."

"Oh, all right." Mr. Volk turned to us. "Let's begin the tour, shall we?"

I watched Jude drive away. Mr. Volk and Elizabeth led us into the building. We entered a spacious lobby with furniture that looked like someone's geometry homework. I wasn't sure if I could actually sit on anything. Dad stared. He might've stared all day if Mom hadn't steered his wheelchair in the right direction. Soon we were walking down a long hall. Paintings lined the walls.

Mr. Volk talked to Mom and Erma about robots, but Dad and I were focused on the paintings, which showed close-ups of different machine parts—intricate clocks, powerful vehicles, and, of course, robots. But all the pictures looked empty, as if they weren't finished yet. I was glad that Dad painted so many people.

Mr. Volk stopped in front of a plain white door and opened it. "This is the design room." Words, numbers, and diagrams in every color were scrawled all over the walls. The only wall without any writing was the one with a bookshelf. The shelf stretched from floor to ceiling. A drafting table stood by the window. Next to it was a cart with wheels. The cart contained pens, pencils, and markers of all kinds and all colors. Large pads of paper stood propped up against the wall. Models of flying machines and submarines hung from the ceiling.

"The walls of this room are coated with a special paint," Mr. Volk said. "You can write on it and erase. Here, try it." Mr. Volk grabbed a can of markers and held it out to us. I chose a blue marker. We began to write.

"I need this paint in my laboratory," Mom said. She had chosen a purple marker. She wrote out a series of equations along a wall.

Dad began sketching on the wall next to the drafting table. He held a marker that drew with a rich red ink. He was drawing a portrait of Elizabeth.

Erma stood next to Mom. She wrote out equations with a bright orange marker. The color was so bright it was hard to look at.

"That is incorrect," said Elizabeth. Her voice made a faint click upon pronunciation of the final *t*.

"Hmph!" Erma was obviously miffed at having been corrected by a robot. "Why don't you do better?" She shoved the marker into Elizabeth's hands.

Elizabeth began to write. Unlike a human, Elizabeth wrote by moving her shoulder instead of her wrist. Her motions were jerky, but her handwriting was straight and evenly spaced, unlike Erma's, which wiggled across the wall.

"I have successfully arrived at a solution." Elizabeth returned the marker to Erma.

Mom looked over Elizabeth's equation. "Astounding," she said. "Mr. Volk, I had no idea your robot could perform such complicated mathematics."

Erma was getting past annoyed and into angry. She stood tall and stiff, and her mouth flattened into a straight line.

"Elizabeth is better at math than I am," Mr. Volk said with a laugh. "But I'm bad at math, so that isn't saying much." Mr. Volk patted the top of Elizabeth's head. "She can't draw, though." He noticed Dad's portrait taking shape next to the drafting table. "I'm not sure if I'll ever be able to erase that."

"I'm glad you like it," Dad said, adding shadows under the chin. Dad says that shading gives a drawing depth. "You and Elizabeth should come to my studio. You could sit for a portrait together. I'm always looking for more people—or androids—to draw."

"Thank you for the offer," Mr. Volk said. "It would be an honor. I will consider it." He held out the can. We put our markers back in.

"Next we'll go to the research room." Mr. Volk led us down a different hall. Here there was no art, but there

were markings on the floor. Perhaps they had been in other places, but I just hadn't noticed them.

"Mr. Volk, what are these pictures on the floor?" I asked.

"Oh, these?" Mr. Volk stopped and pointed to the black and white pattern he was standing on. "Some of my robots don't have optical sensors in their heads like Elizabeth does. Instead they have sensors by their wheels, and they know where they are by reading the codes on the floor."

"Ooh, could you please explain how? Do you mind if I take notes for my research?" Mom took a notebook and pen from her briefcase.

"I'm not sure I can explain it in much detail," Mr. Volk said. "My father developed the system. I just maintain it."

"Well, I'm sure you know more about it than I do," Mom said.

Mr. Volk began explaining the floor codes, pausing only to usher us into a room labeled *Research*.

The research room was overwhelmingly metallic. Desks, chairs, and shelving sparkled against the sunlight streaming through the windows.

Mom continued to ask questions to Mr. Volk. Erma and I began moving around the room. Dad kept careful watch on us.

"Mom's laboratory might not have that special paint, but at least it's not so shiny," Erma said to me. Adding to the shine were metal panels on wheels. The panels could be rearranged to make different spaces within the large room. I sat down on a metal chair in front of a metal desk. The chair was cold and hard.

Mr. Volk showed Mom a book.

"Come on," Erma said, tugging my wrist. "Let's see the rest of this room."

"Don't touch anything," Dad said, following at a distance.

"Don't worry. We won't," Erma said. We walked around a metal panel. We saw another silver table and matching chairs. We turned a corner: a dusty chalkboard. We worked our way through the room, Dad's wheelchair wheels making a sticking sound as they crossed the slick floor.

The room was boring. It contained the same things as Mom's laboratory—filing cabinets, bottles, microscopes, and other tools. Only here they were neatly organized, there were more of them, and they were shinier.

"Doesn't it seem weird to you," Erma said, "that we haven't seen any other people yet?"

"Maybe Mr. Volk gave them the day off."

Erma acted like she didn't hear me. "Why does Mr. Volk have so many desks and chairs if he doesn't have any other people working for him?"

"Maybe they're for his robots. They sure aren't very comfortable to me," I said, trying out a chair.

"It doesn't make sense," Erma said. "Doesn't it seem like something happened to everyone who used to work here?"

I stood up. We wandered past another screen. We stopped and stared. We had never seen one of these in Mom's laboratory—or anywhere else, for that matter.

"What is that?" I asked. "What do you think it's for?"

I didn't hear Dad's wheels. He had probably paused in front of an interesting book.

Erma walked closer to the contraption. It was long and flat like a stiff stretcher for someone to lie down upon. Three pairs of thick leather straps hung from the edges.

"Nick, I think—"

"Look at those." I pointed to sharp tools hanging from a nearby shelf. They looked like surgical instruments.

"Nick, this place is nothing like Mom's laboratory. Mom doesn't have a table like that." Erma pointed to the strange metal bed. "Also, Mom works with other people all of the time."

I began piecing together what Erma said with what I saw. "Are you trying to tell me that Mr. Volk used people for experi—"

"Shh! Not so loud."

"What should we do?" I asked.

"We've got to tell Mom and Dad," Erma said. "For all we know, we might be the next people to go on that table."

I heard Dad's wheels moving again. Mr. Volk's voice came from the other side of the room. "Are you hungry? My chef should have lunch ready. He likes to experiment. Even I don't know what's prepared for today."

15 MECHANICAL MESSENGERS

Mr. Volk's chef was a robot, but I couldn't complain as I ate my spaghetti. When the waiter robot asked if I wanted extra Parmesan cheese, it added just the right amount.

The cafeteria was like a fancy restaurant. I didn't go to those often. Once I had almost gotten my family kicked out of one. All I had wanted to do was help those poor little lobsters in that big tank. They had looked so sad, staring with their beady black eyes, claws forced shut with rubber bands.

Dad asked Mr. Volk about his art collection.

"It was my grandmother's idea to start the collection," Mr. Volk said. "I've always been surrounded by art."

"Do you have a favorite piece?"

Mr. Volk replied with words in a foreign language. I could only guess that was a title, but Dad seemed to know exactly what he had said. Their talk began to sound like one of the lectures at the art museum.

"I'm going to get to the bottom of this," Erma said.

"Not if you just nibble at it." I twisted my fork, wrapping spaghetti around it.

"No, not the spaghetti," Erma said. "This mystery—why Mr. Volk has that metal stretcher in his lab and why there aren't any people here." Erma had barely eaten.

Elizabeth sat next to Mr. Volk. She watched us with her glassy eyes. Apparently robots don't eat. Erma glared at Elizabeth, but the android didn't flinch. Erma nibbled at her food. Even though she was suspicious about Mr. Volk, she had to admit the spaghetti was good.

Once we were done, the waiter robot took our dishes. "Thank you, Simon," Mr. Volk said.

An identical robot came and brought out dessert: generous slices of chocolate cake with equally generous dollops of vanilla ice cream. Upon seeing the sweets, I began to doubt that Mr. Volk was as evil as Erma suspected. I think Erma began to doubt too. She ate the cake with more enthusiasm.

"Thank you, Richard," Mr. Volk said.

"How can you tell them apart?" I asked. "They look exactly the same."

"I know all of my robots by name, Nathan."

"It's Nick," I said.

"Don't you know all of your family and friends by name?"

"But people all look different."

Mr. Volk nodded as if I had proven his point. Perhaps to Mr. Volk, robots did look different. He and Dad resumed their conversation about art. Then an idea hit me.

"Erma," I said, "What if Mr. Volk is a robot?"

"That still doesn't explain the torture device we saw in the research room," Erma said. "Robots can be programmed to do bad things."

I put the final bite of cake into my mouth and tried to make sense of it all.

We continued the tour. Mr. Volk took us through a hall lined with sculptures on pedestals. At first I thought they were sculptures of people, such as the busts of famous musicians we had in the music room at home. Upon getting a closer look, however, I saw that these sculptures were robots.

"This hall features robot designs throughout the history of Volk Enterprises," Mr. Volk said. "These sculptures were once functioning robots."

Plink, who had been silently sitting under my hat the whole time, suddenly leapt off my head. My hat fell to the floor. Plink began tapping on a door with her beak.

I hadn't even noticed the door as we passed. It merged almost seamlessly into the wall.

"Stop," I said, trying to grab Plink. She was hard to grab when her wings were beating so quickly.

Mr. Volk looked more amused than alarmed. "What have we here? Does Norman's little treasure wish to see some treasures of my own?" Mr. Volk pushed on the door. "I don't mind showing you. I merely assumed you wouldn't be interested. After all, you are the descendants of General Newton himself. You might have seen many of these things already."

The door swung inward. Inside was like a small museum. Glass display cases lined the walls. A few smaller display cases stood in the middle. We squeezed in. Dad's wheelchair barely fit into the narrow aisles.

I looked at the displays. They were full of old things like antique pocket watches and rusted automaton parts. There were some framed drawings and a few leather notebooks.

"This is my collection room," Mr. Volk said. "The collection was getting crowded in my house, so I moved some of it here."

"Impressive," Dad said. "I haven't seen one of these since I was a little boy." Dad pointed to an object in the case in front of him. "That's one of Grandfather's first prosthetic arms."

"What's *prosthetic*?" I asked.

"That means it's artificial, not real," Dad explained. "After the war, Grandfather designed this arm for soldiers who had lost their arms in battle. The soldiers could wear the prosthetic arm, and it would be almost like having their real arm back."

"Wow." I pressed against the glass to get a better look. Mr. Volk frowned. I backed away. The arm was made of a thin copper-colored metal. It had joints on all the places a real arm had them—even down to the delicate fingers.

"Unfortunately, the prosthetic arm could never match the strength of a real arm," Dad said. "It was prone to breakage. Once it resulted in the death of the wearer. The chemical used to power it leaked out, poisoning the person's blood. After that, Grandfather stopped making the prosthetic arms. They were recalled and destroyed for safety reasons. A few were preserved to continue research, but the arm never became successful."

"That's only a left arm," Mr. Volk said. "I haven't been able to locate a right arm yet." He sighed wistfully. "I've heard there's even a heart."

"A mechanical heart?" Dad asked.

"Yes, though I've never seen it myself, I've heard other collectors say that General Newton designed a mechanical heart. Are the rumors true? Do you have one for sale?"

Dad only laughed. "My father may have been a genius, but you can't believe everything you hear."

"Well, if you ever come across a genuine Newtonian mechanical heart, please inform me," Mr. Volk said. "I'd do anything to get my hands on one."

"If you don't mind telling, how did you acquire the prosthetic arm?" Dad asked.

Mr. Volk shifted uneasily on his feet. "Suffice it to say that the Volk family has not always adhered to the, umm, how shall I say it . . . the highest ethical standards. I would also like to add that I did not obtain the arm myself. It was in the collection before I inherited it."

"Very well then," Dad said.

Of all the objects in Mr. Volk's display cases, the arm was what interested me most. That is, until I came across a second item that was certainly also one of Grandfather's inventions. I had almost forgotten that I was holding Plink. She began to whistle when I stood in front of a particular display. Inside the glass was another bird. It looked like Plink but different. It was the same size, but it had been painted to resemble a real bird. Feathers were attached to the tips of its metal wings. Even though some of the paint was chipped and some of the feathers were fraying, it made Plink look like a plucked chicken in comparison. Buttons were embedded into its chest. Each button contained a number from zero to nine. I calmed Plink down. She stopped whistling.

Mr. Volk explained, "General Newton used clockwork birds to communicate during the war. Because they were disguised as real birds, they could fly over enemy territory undetected. They could even imitate real bird sounds. If one happened to get caught, the compartment inside, which contained the secret message, would not open unless the right sequence of numbers was pressed." Mr. Volk pointed to the numbers on the bird's chest. "This bird is a standard issue that was manufactured during the war. I have seen rarer models in other collections, but I have never seen yours, Nealson."

"It's Nick," I said.

I looked at the bird in the case. Was this why Plink had tapped on the door? Mr. Volk's bird looked lonely. It was the only item on its shelf. No doubt he had left room in the case for additions to the collection.

"My bird has long been broken," Mr. Volk said. "Not very many survived the war. It's rare to find one intact with its feathers and a decent paint job. If you ever decide to sell yours, Nemo, I would be—"

"Who's this?" Erma pointed to a small picture in a corner display.

Mr. Volk lowered his gaze. I inched closer and to my surprise saw a small sketch of two people—the only other people in the entire building.

"Those are my late parents," Mr. Volk said. "Come now, we'd best continue the tour. I have one last room to show you, and it's rather far away."

Mr. Volk led us out of the room. I placed Plink back onto my head. I covered her with my hat. After a little while, Erma spoke. "You know what I think?" She answered before I could open my mouth. "I think Mr. Volk did something horrible to his parents."

"That's not true," I said. "His parents are fine. They're just going to get here later. That's what he said."

Erma rolled her eyes. "Nick, when Mr. Volk said his parents were late, he meant *late* as in deceased. Dead."

"Oh," I said. "Then why didn't he just say so?"

"Because *late* sounds more polite."

Grown-ups use words in confusing ways.

"But back to what I was saying," Erma said, "Think about it. Doesn't it make sense? First we saw a torture device in the research room. We also know that Mr. Volk has a lot of money. I bet he wanted his parents gone so he could have all their money to himself and—"

"Stop, stop." I said. "That can't be true."

"I'd watch out if I were you, Nick. You have something Mr. Volk wants." She pointed to my hat, indicating

Plink underneath. "He's already admitted that his family hasn't always behaved ethically. Who knows how far he'll go to get what he wants?"

"I'm not listening," I said. We had fallen behind, and I raced to catch up.

Mom had begun to talk to Mr. Volk about the energy source he used to fuel his robots. "It must cost a fortune to keep them all running," she said.

"Oh, it's not as expensive as you might think."

"What do you use?" Mom asked.

"I'm no scientist, but I'm curious too," Dad said.

Mr. Volk smiled. "I'm sorry, but it's a family secret. I'm afraid I can't tell you."

16 MANUFACTURING

We arrived at the manufacturing room. "It gets noisy, so I'll give you each a pair of earmuffs." Mr. Volk passed around a box. The earmuffs were grown-up sized. I had to hold onto mine with my hands. I slid them around the back of my head so I wouldn't have to take off my hat. Mr. Volk pressed buttons on each side of Elizabeth's head instead of giving her earmuffs. This must have quieted her hearing.

Walking into the manufacturing room was like walking into a different building. This room was filled with machinery—conveyor belts, presses, a cutting machine, and, of course, robots. I couldn't tell what they were doing, but they sure were busy.

We stood on a walkway high above the ground floor. The walkway spanned the entire edge of the room so we could see everything without touching the ground. The only way to get down was the metal staircase on the far end of the room.

"Today my machines are working on a—" Mr. Volk's voice was cut off by a sawing sound. I watched the robots scurry across the floor. These robots didn't look like Plink or like Elizabeth. They were different shapes and sizes. Some were round. Some were pincers attached to arms. Mom and Dad tried to listen to what Mr. Volk said. I watched the robots. They weren't moving on wheels or walking around by themselves. Instead, the panels on the floor moved, carrying them along. It was like those sliding tile puzzles that Dad had bought for me and Erma. I never could put mine together, but Erma could complete hers in five minutes.

Suddenly I saw a robot that looked different. It darted onto the floor trying to avoid the other machines. Then I realized it wasn't a robot at all. It was Erma!

"Erma!" I shouted. She didn't hear. Neither did Mom, Dad, or Mr. Volk. I ran to my parents. I tugged Dad's sleeve and pointed frantically to the ground floor.

"What is it, Nick?" Dad asked. I couldn't hear him, but I could read his lips.

"Erma's down there!" I shouted. This time my voice carried over the noise.

Mr. Volk sprang into action. He darted down the stairs and ran to a large lever. He grasped it with both hands and tried to pull. Elizabeth saw him struggling and ran around the walkway until she stood almost above him. She leapt over the railing. She landed like a cat right by his side. She helped him pull. Together they forced the lever down.

Mr. Volk pressed buttons on a panel in the wall. My eyes tracked Erma's movements. She was heading toward a door painted with yellow and black stripes. In red letters above and below it read, "Danger! Top Secret!"

Mom and Dad came up to the railing, each on either side of me. We watched helplessly as Erma weaved in and out between robots. She barely dodged a swinging arm. We all shouted at her to stop. I took another look at the glowing panel that Mr. Volk was working on. Was it a small version of the floor layout?

Perhaps Erma thought of this as another puzzle game. She always asks me to play them with her. I'm not very good at them, but this time she was playing against Mr. Volk. And instead of trying to block her, he seemed to be keeping her out of harm's way.

"Erma, stop this instant!" Dad used what I call his *general voice*, how I imagined Grandfather sounded when he barked orders on the battlefield.

"I won't stop!" Erma said. "There's something terrible behind that door. I'll prove it!" As she spoke, Erma wasn't paying attention to where she went. Her shoelace got caught in a moving panel. She fell, the panel dragging her along. She tried pulling off her shoe, but the laces yanked into a knot, tightening around her foot. She looked up. Ahead loomed a machine that was cutting sheets of metal. We watched in horror as Erma inched closer to the blade.

Mr. Volk turned and locked eyes with Elizabeth. He nodded and pointed to Erma, who was now screaming over the noise.

Elizabeth ran onto the manufacturing floor. She dodged other machines and stepped in all the right places. She rammed against Erma, forcing her off the moving pathway.

There was no more time. The metal cutter crashed down on Elizabeth. It didn't open.

I heard a muffled boom. Sparks flew from the control panel where Mr. Volk stood. Smoke poured from the wall. Everything stopped. For the first time since we had entered the room, it fell completely silent.

I wiped my sweating brow with an equally sweaty hand. My hat felt out of place. I repositioned it and felt Plink's head poking out from underneath. She had seen everything.

The smoke cleared. A black liquid had puddled around Elizabeth. Mr. Volk unfastened his white cloak and cast it over the mangled machine. The liquid seeped into the cloak, ruining the fabric.

"Can you stand?" Mr. Volk held out his left hand to Erma. She took it and shakily stood. Mr. Volk led her up the stairs and delivered her safely back to us.

"Mr. Volk, your hand," Mom cried.

I looked at his right hand. It was badly burned.

"Do you remember the way to the entrance?" Mr. Volk sounded much more at ease than he appeared. "Do you mind showing yourselves out? This tour has taken longer than anticipated. Your butler is likely waiting for you."

Dad tried to speak. An apology sputtered out of his mouth. Mr. Volk turned his back on him. Dad fell silent. We walked to the door. I took one last glance at Mr. Volk before leaving. Had the smoke caused his eyes to water, or was he trying to hold back tears?

17 STRANGE RUMORS

"Erma, what were you thinking?" Mom said. The car began to move.

"I wanted to—"

"You weren't thinking," Mom said.

"Yes, I was," Erma protested. "Doesn't Mr. Volk seem suspicious?"

"That man just saved your life."

"We will discuss this at home," Dad said. "Until then, let's try to enjoy what's left of this summer day."

We remained quiet throughout the rest of the ride.

Calla smiled when she saw us come in. Addie began to spout baby babble. Calla's smile faded once she saw our glum faces. Addie stopped her babbling.

Dad spoke. "You caused a lot of trouble today, Erma. Not just for Mr. Volk, but for your own family as well."

I began walking to my room. I didn't need to hear Dad's words to Erma—that was between him and her—but it was kind of hard to not hear them.

"As part of your punishment, I forbid you to participate in the Grand Fair," Dad said.

"But Daaaaad! How can I win if I don't compete?"

"Erma!" Dad roared. Today he would not tolerate that.

I darted up the stairs.

I didn't see Mr. Volk for a long time.

"Why are you concerned about him?" Elliot asked one day. "Didn't you say he always wanted Plink? You should be glad he's not bothering you anymore."

I told Elliot everything. It was my first time telling anyone.

Elliot was silent for a bit. Then he asked, "What do you think he did with Elizabeth?"

"Maybe he could repair her," I said. "Plink was in pieces when I found her."

"Did you at least apologize to Mr. Volk?" Elliot asked.

"We sent a letter of apology," I said. "We sent a check, too, to try to help cover the cost of the damage. The check was returned to us, but we didn't get the note back. I hope he's OK. He burned his hand pretty badly."

Several classmates had been eavesdropping. When I finished the story, people clamored out questions.

"So he's not an evil genius scientist?"

"You didn't see his plans to conquer the world with robots?"

"You mean he doesn't collect the brains of students who make low grades? *Whew!* I don't feel so scared about the next math test!"

I answered the questions as best I could. Most were answered with a simple *no*.

SOLOMON'S STORY 18

Every autumn our friends, the Cedrics, host a big party at their house. Unlike some parties, the Cedrics always invite children as well as grown-ups. I'm happy to go because Mrs. Cedric stocks the dessert table full of cakes, pies, and cookies.

At this year's party, as usual, Mom, Dad, and Erma all found other geniuses to talk to. I was glad to have Plink for company, but she couldn't exactly talk. I wandered around, munching on a cookie. Then I saw him.

He was sitting alone at a table in the garden. It was cold out, and it was getting dark, but he didn't seem to mind. He wore a heavy brown cloak and a matching top hat.

I stepped outside and walked up to him. "Hello, Mr. Volk."

"Ah, if it isn't Nigel."

"Nick," I corrected.

"Aren't you cold?" he asked. "You should be inside with everyone else."

"I'm OK," I said, but I was a little cold. "Why aren't you inside with everyone else?"

"I don't really like parties. Too many people. I only come to the Cedrics' parties. My parents loved the Cedrics and their parties."

I glanced at his hands, but they were covered with gloves.

"Where's Elizabeth?" I asked.

"I was unable to repair her. Her core, the mechanism that is like her heart, was too badly damaged."

"What if you had a mechanical heart?"

"So it exists after all?" Mr. Volk asked.

"I don't know," I said, "but I can help you look for it. The attic at home is full of old things. It's where I found Plink. Maybe we can get some clues."

"That sounds splendid," Mr. Volk said.

"Also, one other thing." I found myself holding my hand out. Plink rested on my palm. "Here," I said. "She's yours. You've always been asking to purchase—"

Mr. Volk paused, looking at Plink. Then he shook his head. "Do you seriously think a member of the Volk family needs a charitable donation?"

"Maybe think about it like a trade," I suggested. "You gave up one of your robots to save my sister, and now I'm giving you one of my robots."

Plink turned her head and looked at me. She looked worried.

"No, it's not a fair trade," Mr. Volk said. "Elizabeth was unlike any other robot. My parents designed her and had her created specifically for me. She was one of a kind. And so is Plink. Plink will mean more to you than she could ever mean to me, and Elizabeth will mean more to me than she could ever mean to you."

"You're right," I said. "I can't trade Plink." I lowered my hand and held Plink close. "I never got to meet Grandfather, but Plink reminds me of him."

"Elizabeth reminded me of my parents. It's been a few years since they passed on, but I still miss them. Silly, isn't it?"

"I don't think so," I said. "After all, it's not like you're a robot yourself . . . are you?"

Mr. Volk stared at me.

"I'm sorry." I wished I could take back my words.

"Did you just ask if I were a robot?"

"Well, yes. Some of my classmates insist that you are. Even some of the geniuses at Erma's school say that you are."

"Please tell. What else do the children say about me?"

"You really want to know?"

"Yes. I am very interested."

I told Mr. Volk all the rumors I could remember: that he collected students' brains if they didn't make high test scores, that all his robots had once been human, that he was planning to take over the world, and more.

After hearing the rumors, he wasn't sad or angry like I expected him to be. Instead he laughed. He laughed like a little kid. And when I heard him laugh, he didn't seem so scary.

"I had no idea you all found me so interesting. Now, Nick, could you please do me a favor?"

I was so shocked that he had gotten my name right that I almost forgot to say yes.

"I would appreciate it if you could clear up the rumor about me murdering my own parents." He shuddered. "But . . . but maybe leave the rumor about me being a robot. I sort of like that one. Don't lie; just don't say anything when it comes up. Let them keep guessing, all right?" Mr. Volk winked.

"OK," I said with a grin. "I won't say anything about that one."

"If I ask you that favor, I suppose I should tell you the truth. Would you like to know my story? It may take a moment to tell."

"Yes," I said. "I would like to hear it."

Mr. Volk told me his story. He told me about his parents. They had tried to steer the company in the right direction, but they had died in a tragic accident. Mr. Volk inherited Volk Enterprises. He had trusted the executives who had worked for his parents to help him run the company, but instead they had tried to steal it from him. He fired them all. He fired every human working at Volk Enterprises. It hadn't been easy, but he and his robots had taken care of the business ever since. "Robots don't have ambition," Mr. Volk said. "They don't steal things."

"Sounds lonely though," I said. So many assumptions about Mr. Volk had been wrong. I didn't understand everything about him, but I now knew enough to be sure he wasn't the person I thought he had been.

Mr. Volk picked up his plate from the table. A few colorful sprinkles were scattered across it. "Did you like the cookies, Nick?"

I realized I had a cookie sticking out of my pocket. "Yes, sir. They were good as always."

"I will go and get some then. Have you tried the cake?"

"No, sir."

"You should try it. It's better than what my robots can make." Mr. Volk rose from his seat. "Would you care to come inside with me?"

"Sure, Mr. Volk."

"By the way, Nick, you may call me Solomon," Mr. Volk said. "After all, that's what all my robots call me."

Part Three

THE SEWING MACHINE 19

Elliot came to my house after school. We worked on homework together.

"I'm doing my research project on toilets," Elliot said.

"Did Mrs. Bonswoggle really let you do your project on that?" I asked.

"She sure did. What are you doing your project on, Nick?"

"I'm doing it on Plink, of course." Plink sat on my shoulder and chirped.

"This is going to be fun," Elliot said.

"You mean you're actually excited about something that isn't a comic book?" Erma walked by on the way up to her room. She carried a stack of books, likely for her classical literature class.

"I get excited about lots of things," Elliot said, "like action figures and gumball machines."

Erma shook her head and continued walking.

"I hope I can find enough information for my project," I said. "I don't know anything about Plink. She came with a notebook of drawings, and Solomon told me about the mechanical messengers, the other birds like her, but I can't find library books or anything."

"Well, you had better look harder," Elliot said. "We only have a few weeks to work on this project."

"Back to math," I said. "Are you done with question eight yet?"

A loud whirring came from down the hall.

"Oh, no! It's eating all the fabric!"

"Make it stop. Make it stop!"

Besides Elliot, Solomon had also come over. Since the Cedrics' party, he's become a regular visitor of ours. It's like having an older brother. Everyone in the family calls him Solomon except for Erma, who still calls him Mr. Volk, and Addie, who calls him Ollo because that's the best she can say. Mom and Dad were renovating Solomon's antique sewing machine. It's been an ongoing project. Elliot and I finished our math homework amidst some unusual mechanical sounds.

"I should get going." Elliot threw his books and pencils into his book bag. I spotted the colorful cover of a comic book sticking out. “Tomorrow I’m going to the museum. Would you like to come?”

“Sure, but let me ask my parents first.” I ran down the hall and soon came back. “They said yes.”

“Great! I’ll meet you in the lobby around 10 a.m.”

“Sounds good.”

Elliot grinned. “The special exhibition is on toilets. I can’t wait!”

“I’ll tell Jude you’re ready to go home.”

“I don’t mind walking home. It’s a nice day.”

“But you live far away. I’ll go get him.” I left Elliot in the living room. When I returned with Jude, Elliot had gone. I glanced outside. He was already down the road.

“Should I go fetch him with the car?” Jude asked.

“No, he’ll be all right. He walks everywhere.”

“I’m interested to see how the sewing machine is progressing.” Jude disappeared down the hall.

I sat on the couch. “Maybe we should look at the library again,” I told Plink. She let out a chirp that sounded like a sigh. “If only you could talk, then I could get all my research directly from you.”

I heard whirring behind me. The sewing machine flew into the living room! Mom and Solomon came running after it.

“You didn’t tell me you were going to make it fly,” Solomon said.

"Isn't it wonderful?" Mom said. The sewing machine hovered around the room with a tiny propeller at the top. Plink flew up to investigate. Dad came out to look.

"You can make anything fly, can't you?" Solomon said.

"That flying mechanism is mostly clockwork," Mom said.

"Clockwork? You mean like Plink?" I asked.

"Yes, like Plink." Mom sat down next to me on the couch. Plink, having decided the sewing machine was not a threat, landed on Mom's hand. Mom ran a finger over the hole in Plink's back. "Don't you have to wind her up with a key?"

"Yes," I said. "Every week, or she stops working."

The sewing machine landed on the floor. The propeller folded and withdrew into an inside compartment. Solomon walked over to it. "You know what else is clockwork?" Solomon asked.

"Umm . . . clocks?"

Solomon laughed. "Well, yes, but I meant the mechanical heart." He took a small folder from inside his coat. "I traded some rare books to get this." Solomon opened the folder. Inside was a single tattered drawing—a sketch of a human heart made of gears and metal tubes.

"So it does exist?"

"No one is certain yet," Solomon said. "No collector or museum curator has ever seen a real one, but I thought that maybe if I studied pictures carefully enough, I could make one. Maybe not fit for a human, but good enough for an android."

I thought about Elizabeth. "You should come with me to the museum tomorrow. Elliot wants to look at toilets, but we can look for clockwork things."

"The museum?" Solomon put the folder away and picked up his sewing machine. "Some of its items came from the Volk collection, you know. I wouldn't mind seeing them again."

I told him the time to meet.

"I will plan to join you. Now, however, I should get going." He turned to Mom and Dad. "Thank you for your help with this." He held up the sewing machine.

"But it still doesn't sew," Dad said.

"That's OK. I'll bring it back next time. Thanks again." Solomon waved goodbye and was off.

20 THE SPECIAL EXHIBITION

The next day we met at the museum as planned. Solomon wanted to look at sewing machines, but Elliot insisted on looking at toilets first. He grabbed a pamphlet about the toilet exhibition.

I looked around the lobby. I saw some new displays. One featured uniforms from the Last War. Before I could get closer, Elliot took me in the opposite direction. "Toilets first," he said.

Previous special exhibitions had included medieval armor, dinosaur fossils, and mummies, but today the hall was filled with toilets.

"This is the best special exhibition ever!" Elliot took out a notebook and pen. "I'm going to take notes for my research project." He read the display plaque in front of a primitive-looking wooden toilet. He began writing in his notebook.

Solomon and I wandered through the hall. Solomon looked bored. Then he halted in front of a shimmering white toilet. Sculpted wings wrapped around the bowl. The handle to flush took the shape of a dainty silver feather. Solomon stared at the toilet like Dad stared at art.

Elliot eventually made his way to us. He showed me his notebook. He had gotten a lot of notes and even a few sketches. He noticed the winged toilet. "I wonder what weirdo designed that?"

"I did," Solomon said.

"What?"

Elliot and I read the display plaque. Sure enough, the description stated that it had been designed at Volk Enterprises. The plaque also described it as "impractical," "unpopular," and "an embarrassment for the otherwise successful company."

"It was a bad idea," Solomon said. "I ordered my robots to destroy all of them, but it appears they missed one. Hmph! You can't trust robots to do everything." Solomon adjusted his cloak over his narrow shoulders. "I am going to talk to the curator about this. I shall purchase this toilet and destroy it myself."

Once Solomon had set his mind on getting something, little could be done to stop him. "To the museum offices," he announced. Elliot and I could have gone off by ourselves, but we were too curious to see what Solomon would do next.

On our way to the offices, we walked past other displays. I glanced at bug collections, gemstones, and antique furniture. Then came the Hall of Warfare. Plink shot off my shoulder and into the exhibit.

"Hey, wait for us!" I ran after her. Elliot followed. Solomon suddenly became less interested in his mission to obtain the toilet. He followed too.

The Hall of Warfare was dimly lit. It contained weapons, uniforms, and battle dioramas. Patriotic music played in the background.

"Who's he?" Elliot asked, pointing to a picture.

"That's my grandfather, General Newton." I said. "That's what he looked like during the war. He was young then."

"He looks like you," Elliot said, "or you look like him."

Grandfather had the same brown hair and brown eyes that I had. Our faces had the same shape. In this picture he looked sad. He looked much happier in the portrait in my living room.

Plink chirped, not to be ignored. She stood atop a glass case under the painting. Inside was another clockwork bird.

"It's like your bird, Solomon," I said, "sort of. This one's orange. I've never seen a real bird with orange feathers like that. They look like they could glow in the dark."

"It says that this model was used for testing." Elliot read from the card attached to the case. I told Elliot about Solomon's mechanical messenger.

"Mine was meant to stay hidden," Solomon said, "but this one was meant to be found."

"I wonder why some of the numbers on its chest are pressed in?" Elliot pointed to the chest panel, which displayed the numbers zero through nine. The one, five, six, and zero were pressed in.

"Elliot, could you copy that into your notebook?" I asked.

Elliot took out his notebook. He drew a diagram of the bird's chest and shaded in the pressed numbers.

"I don't see why this is important." Elliot finished shading in the last number. "Anyone could've pushed those buttons."

"Come to think of it," Solomon mused, "my bird also has some numbers pressed in."

Then I told them about a chest I had found in the attic. "I found a wooden chest pushed all the way in the back. I couldn't open it. It has three locks—brown, orange, and blue. Each lock has numbers arranged just like they are on this bird: zero through nine. What if we press the numbers on the orange bird into the orange lock?"

Elliot tore the page from his notebook and handed it to me. "You should try it."

"Thanks." I took the paper, folded it carefully, and slipped it into my pocket. "Solomon, could you check the numbers on your brown bird?"

"Certainly."

"Well, what are we waiting for?" Elliot asked. "Mr. Solomon, go get those numbers. Nick, you punch that code into the lock!"

"Jude isn't picking me up until noon," I said. "What else should we look at in the museum?"

Elliot thought a moment. "Bugs."

"Sewing machines." Solomon said.

"Clockwork stuff." I suddenly remembered my own research project. Plink flitted onto my shoulder. We left the Hall of Warfare and headed to other displays. After seeing bugs, sewing machines, and clockwork stuff, Elliot couldn't leave until he had gone to the gift shop.

"Wow, look at these. Aren't they great?" Elliot pointed out a plastic cup filled with pencils. A toilet-shaped eraser topped each one. Elliot dug into his pockets, but he didn't have any money. "Rats," he said. "I really wanted one."

"I'll get one for you," Solomon offered.

"Really?" Elliot's face brightened. "Mr. Solomon, you're the best."

"It's no big deal. Which color would you like?" Solomon took the cup of pencils off the shelf and lowered it so we could get a better look.

We walked out of the gift shop each with our own toilet-topped pencil.

"Mr. Solomon, you never talked to the curator about that toilet," Elliot said.

"I've decided to let it be," Solomon said. "Others may mock the design, but after seeing it again, I'm still proud of it. I think it deserves to be part of the exhibit."

21 BELLINGHAM UNIVERSITY

Once home, Plink and I raced up to the attic. I climbed the ladder and found the chest. Plink perched on my head. I kneeled and entered the code into the orange lock. But as soon as I had punched it in, the keys popped back up.

"Maybe I'm wrong," I said. "Maybe the locks don't match the birds."

On Monday when I came home from school, I saw Solomon's car in the driveway. I poked my head into the science lab. Elliot followed behind. Mom worked on Solomon's sewing machine. Dad drew something on large sheets of paper.

"How was your day?" Mom glanced up from her work.

"It was okay. I didn't do so well on my science test though. I got a C."

"Was that the one I helped you study for?" Solomon asked.

"Yes," I said.

"Sorry. I'm not the best with science," Solomon admitted, "but if you ever need help with business management—"

"It's not your fault. I didn't memorize all the parts of the cell liked I needed to. I should've studied more, I guess."

"There's still time to raise your grade," Dad said. "We know you'll do your best."

"I will," I said. "Next time, I'll study even more. Hey, Elliot, what grade did you get?"

"I don't like to talk about my grades."

"Sorry." I quickly changed the subject. "Solomon, did you get the code from your clockwork bird?"

"Yes. As I had thought, some of the keys were punched in. I remember when I first had bought the bird, I tried to pry them out, but they wouldn't budge. Maybe they're glued in place. It's a shame. It distracts from the design." He handed me a paper. Solomon had drawn a diagram indicating which numbers were punched in: one, three, six, and two.

"Have you ever seen a blue clockwork bird?" I asked.

"A blue one?" Solomon repeated. "I haven't, but it would be a nice addition to the collection."

"A blue one would be pretty," Dad said. "I wonder how Plink would look in blue?"

Plink chirped indignantly.

"Don't worry, Plink," I said. "We're looking for a bird that's already blue."

"I could ask my dad," Elliot said. "He knows all about stuff like that."

"Umm, OK," I said. "Let me know how that goes."

"Why don't we ask him together? I'm sure he'd like to meet you."

The next day I found myself visiting Bellingham University. "Why didn't you tell me your dad was a history professor?"

"You didn't ask."

Bellingham University was where Erma wanted to go to college. She said it was a very prestigious school. I think that meant expensive.

Elliot walked across campus like it was his backyard. "Maybe people will think we're new students. We can pretend we're geniuses attending Bellingham University at only ten years old. Oh, hi, Professor Dickinson. Have you seen my dad?"

"He was leaving his office for his four o' clock class. You had better hurry if you want to catch him on his way there."

"Thanks, Prof."

"You're welcome, Elliot."

Elliot waved goodbye to the professor with one hand and cleaned out his ear with the pinky of the other. The professor continued walking, shaking his head but smiling.

Class had already begun when we arrived.

"I'd be dead if I interrupted a lecture," Elliot said. "This is his last class for the day. Let's wait outside until it's over." Elliot sat on a bench in the hall and pulled a comic book from his book bag.

I peeked through the narrow window on the door. A man in a blue jacket and mismatched socks stood at the front of the room. He spoke loudly. I could hear everything.

"He's talking about Grandfather," I said.

"Of course," Elliot said. "This is the military history class." Elliot turned back to his comic book. A giant monster stomped across the cover.

I listened intently to Elliot's dad. He lectured about a battle I had never heard of, emphasizing the role of a ruthless enemy from Oreshaffe named Draicot.

"But despite Lieutenant General Draicot's excellent strategy," Professor Twain said, "he was outmaneuvered by General Newton's superior military technology. After Newton's multiple victories, Thauma had the upper hand for the rest of the war."

A student raised his hand. "I thought the Battle of Rosewater was the decisive victory in the war."

"Some scholars say so," Professor Twain said, "but I argue for the Battle of Fog Lane. I think stopping Draicot was the key to Newton's final triumph."

Another student raised her hand. "Professor, what happened to Lieutenant General Draicot? Did he get killed or captured? I don't recall reading about him in any of the following battles."

"Good question, Susan," Professor Twain said. "Historians are divided as to what happened to Draicot. Most say he died at Fog Lane. Others argue that he was captured by General Newton. Still others say he continued to fight. He is quite mysterious."

The bell rang.

"Well, class, we will continue the story next time. Don't forget about your reading assignment, and I trust you are making good progress on your research papers."

I scrambled out of the way as the students left. A few stayed behind to ask questions. After the room cleared, Elliot and I went in.

"Hi, Dad," Elliot said.

"Hello, Elliot. What brings you to the university today?"

"Show him, Nick," Elliot said.

I took off my hat, revealing Plink underneath.

"Ooh, a mechanical messenger! Those are rare treasures. May I take a closer look?" The professor tried to touch Plink, but she darted away.

"It works!" Professor Twain exclaimed. "I've never seen one that still functions."

"Have you ever seen a blue one?" I asked.

"A blue one? Hmm." Professor Twain cleaned out his ear with his pinky finger. He looked at the books on his shelf.

"Nick is General Newton's grandson," Elliot said.

Professor Twain yanked his finger from his ear did a swift about-face. "Are you pulling my leg? Elliot, why didn't you tell me your friend was the general's grandson?"

"You didn't ask."

Professor Twain turned to me and smiled. "You know, Elliot's told me a lot about you, but I never realized you were related to General Newton. He is one of my heroes."

"He's one of mine too," I said.

Professor Twain pulled out several books. "Let's look at these."

Elliot sighed. "Book research is so boring."

Plink must have noticed that I felt comfortable around the professor. She landed on his shoulder and sang.

"Oh, ho. What a strange one this is. Mechanical messengers weren't made to sing. Where did you find this?"

I told Professor Twain what I knew about Plink.

"She must be one of a kind." The professor sat down at his desk and opened a book. "Let's see. This book contains photos and drawings related to the war. Some of these images haven't been published anywhere else."

As Professor Twain flipped through the book, a black and white photo caught my eye. "Who's he?"

"That would be Lieutenant General Draicot. Brilliant strategist. Too bad he was on the wrong side. He doesn't appear in many photos, and as far as I know, he never sat for a portrait. He was a logical, practical, stoic man. Looks the part, doesn't he?"

The picture was grainy, but the face looked familiar. Professor Twain turned to a chapter on General Newton's inventions. He flipped past cannons, guns, and tanks and landed on the page about mechanical messengers.

"There's the blue one." Elliot touched a small picture in the bottom corner. "It says that the blue one is a prototype, whatever that means."

"That means it was made before the others. It wasn't the final design," Professor Twain explained. "It must be rare indeed."

I squinted my eyes at the tiny words to the side of the photo. "It says, 'Photo courtesy of the State Museum, the Volk Collection, and the Ihara Collection.'"

"There's your answer," Elliot said. "The museum has the orange one, and Mr. Solomon has the brown one, so that means Ihara, whoever he is, must have the blue one."

Professor Twain looked up Ihara in the book's index. Nothing.

"I've never heard of an Ihara," I said.

"Ask Mr. Solomon," Elliot said. "He's a collector. He might know."

"Solomon as in Solomon Volk?" Professor Twain asked. "You're friends with a robot?"

Apparently even professors weren't immune to the silly rumors about Solomon.

22 SOLOMON'S RIVAL

"Ihara is a collector I avoid," Solomon said.

"But we've got to try," I said.

Solomon sighed. "I will see what I can do. I will have you know, however, that Ihara is my rival. She has the habit of appearing at the same auctions I attend, and she bids on the same items. She has impeccable taste. I'll grant her that."

The next day Solomon informed me that he had written to Ihara. Now all we could do was wait. Mom and Dad continued work on Solomon's sewing machine. It could now fire needles like bullets.

"But it still can't sew," Solomon said.

"I think it's perfect," Elliot declared.

Elliot and I worked on our research projects. Elliot had collected a surprising amount of information on toilets, but I barely had enough information about clockwork.

A week later Solomon came to the house with a lavender envelope. "Look. Ihara wrote back."

"Well, what did she say?" I asked.

"She says we are welcome to come and look at her collection, but there is one condition."

"What is it?"

"We aren't allowed to touch anything."

"And if we do?"

"The letter doesn't specify. It just says *or else*."

"What are we waiting for?" Elliot said. "Let's go."

"I'm sorry, Elliot, but I didn't inform Ihara of anyone else coming except for myself, Nick, and Plink."

"Aww. Nick, you had better tell me everything about it."

That weekend Jude drove me to the first purple mansion I had ever seen. Solomon was waiting next to his own car, which now had wings.

"Remember, don't touch anything," Solomon said as we walked up to the door. "The same goes for you, Plink." Solomon pressed a button next to the door.

"Who goes there?" A voice came from a dragon-shaped speaker unit.

Solomon leaned closer to the dragon. "Solomon Volk, Nicholas Newton, and Plink."

"Proceed," the dragon said. The door swung inward. We went through, and the door closed behind us.

We found ourselves in a room that looked like a museum having a yard sale. Objects stood atop furniture. Items were crammed into cabinets and overflowed from shelving. Still others were strewn across the floor. The scene was the total opposite of Solomon's tidy collection room. This room smelled like old books and incense.

"Watch your step," Solomon said. I felt like I had walked into a minefield, and Solomon's warning made me extra fidgety. I thrust my hands into my pockets to resist the mounting desire to touch everything. Plink flew up and began circling over a heap of items on a table.

"I think she's found something," I said. "Good work, Plink."

We tiptoed over. "I don't see a blue bird," I said. Plink swooped down low, nearly touching a small, silver object.

Solomon craned his neck to get a better look. "It's a pocket watch."

"Oh." I walked around to the other side. "It looks similar to Jude's watch. That's not what we're after, Plink."

Plink went off again. She began chirping in front of a wooden display case. It contained several guns. I recognized them from books about the Last War.

"Grandfather designed these."

"Not only that," Solomon said, "these are prototypes. And not only are they rare, these are in great condition."

"Plink, that's still not quite it," I said. Plink flew off in a different direction. We followed. She shot up to the highest shelf in the room. Was that a sliver of blue hanging over the edge?

"Maybe that's it." I turned to Solomon. "Can you see the numbers on its chest?"

Solomon was a small man. He looked even smaller today without his cloak and hat. "No, I'm afraid I can't see them." He stood on tiptoe. He began to jump up and down. "It's a bird, all right, but I can't get a good look at the numbers."

"I know," I said. "Lift me up onto your shoulders."

"What? I don't think that's a good idea."

"Come on, Solomon. We've come this far. We can't give up now."

"All right. Up you go." Solomon grunted as he lifted me. "Oof! Can you see it now?"

"It's the blue bird, all right."

"And the numbers?"

"One, two, three, zero," I said.

"OK, good. I'm going to put you down now."

Getting down was harder than going up. I slipped, Solomon lost his balance, and we tumbled to the floor.

Fortunately, we landed on cushions. Unfortunately, that meant we were touching something.

"Bravo, Solomon, bravo." A cabinet twirled around. An elderly lady stood on the other side. "I knew you would touch something if I set the bird up there."

"You mean this was just a big trick?" Solomon sprang to his feet and then helped me to mine.

"How else could I get you to talk to your own grandmother?" the lady said. "And this is your consequence for touching something in my collection: you must come in to where it isn't so messy and have some tea with me."

She looked at me, her dark eyes shining. "You must be Nick. Are you looking out for my grandson? He's always been trouble, you know." She laughed.

I looked at her and then at Solomon. My face must have told them I needed an explanation.

"Nick, this is my grandmother, Mrs. Francine Ihara. Grandma, this is Nick Newton."

Mrs. Ihara ushered us into the kitchen. "Let's talk over something warm to drink," she said, "and I'm sorry you had to see my collection in such chaos. I'm in the middle of reorganizing. It's usually slightly less messy."

The kitchen looked like it belonged to a small country cottage instead of a huge purple mansion. Cross-stitch samplers decorated the walls. Gingham curtains hung over the windows. Matching pillows sat in chairs around a small, round table. The room was warm and smelled like baking. Mrs. Ihara poured us cups of hot tea. We sat down together.

"I've invited Solomon over many times, but he's always declined," Mrs. Ihara told me. "I wrote letters, and all I received in return were notes obviously written by one of his robots."

"I'm sorry, Grandma. But after Mom and Dad died and after everything that happened with the company, I guess I didn't want to be around people at all."

"Oh, believe me. I understand, dear. I felt the same way when Oswald passed on." Mrs. Ihara looked at a painting on the wall. It showed her younger self standing close to a handsome man in a tweed jacket. "Oswald would have helped you run the company. I apologize that I could not do more for you."

"Don't blame yourself," Solomon said.

"But we're all here now," Mrs. Ihara said, "and now is all we can do anything about."

Solomon managed to smile. Somehow I knew this wouldn't be the last time we would visit the purple mansion.

GRAND OPENING 23

"We have all three codes," I said. "There's only one thing left to do."

"I know. Eat some cheese." Elliot declared. He pulled a wedge of cheese out of his book bag and bit into it like an apple.

"Umm . . . no," I said. "How about we open the chest in the attic?"

"That's exciting too," Elliot said, mumbling through bites of cheese.

"What are we waiting for? Let's go. I think we need to enter all three codes at the same time."

"Is Mr. Solomon coming?" Elliot asked.

"Oh, I forgot. He's away at an auction. Something about a tank for sale. He'll be gone for a few days."

"I can't wait that long."

"Neither can I. We'll open it ourselves. We'll find a way."

As always, Jude was waiting with the car. Elliot and I took the back seats.

"It's about time. We've been sitting here forever." Erma sat in the front seat. Jude had picked her up from school first. Jude started the car and began to drive. Elliot continued eating his cheese.

"What's that smell?" Erma asked.

"Cheese. Want some?" Elliot pulled off a chunk. "I didn't bite this part."

"No, that's gross." Erma wrinkled her nose.

"Nick?" Elliot shoved the cheese closer to my face.

"Uh, sure." I took the cheese from Elliot. I popped it into my mouth. It was pretty good.

"You're so gross," Erma said.

Jude parked the car in front of the house. Elliot and I got out, but Erma stayed firmly in place. "Jude, I want to go shopping."

"Certainly, Erma," Jude replied. He and Erma drove off.

I led Elliot up into the attic. "It's right here," I said.

Elliot knocked over the old dress form. Dust swirled around, turning the attic into a discolored snow globe. We coughed. When the dust cleared, I showed Elliot the chest with the locks. "I think we need to punch the codes in at the same time."

"But there are only two of us."

"We've each got two hands. I'll press two codes in at once." I laid the codes on top of the chest. "On the count of three, we punch in the codes." I placed each hand over a lock. Elliot took his place at the third. "One . . . two . . . three!"

Punching in two codes at the same time was harder than I thought. The locks reset and refused to open. Plink pecked at my hand. "Ouch, Plink. Stop that." I shooed her away, but she continued to peck at me. "Let's try that again. One . . . two . . . three."

Punching in two codes at once was even more difficult with Plink pecking at my hands. The locks didn't open.

"Let me try to do two," Elliot said. Plink began attacking him. "Ouch! Ow!"

"Plink, that's enough." I grabbed her, put her in a rusty birdcage, and latched the door. She began screeching, but I did my best to ignore her. I took my place back at the chest.

"One . . . two . . . three!" Elliot and I punched in the codes, but the locks were still tight.

"I wish Solomon had come," I said.

"Let's ask someone else," Elliot suggested. "Your mom and dad are home, right?"

"But Dad is in a wheelchair," I said. "He can't come up here."

"Oh, that's right."

"But maybe Mom or Calla could help."

We climbed down and walked to Mom's laboratory. A Do Not Disturb sign hung on the door. We heard an explosion from within followed by the smell of rotten eggs.

"Let's leave her alone for now," I said.

We heard classical music coming from Dad's studio. The stench of rotten eggs mingled strangely with the pleasant sounds. We continued on and came to the nursery.

"Calla, could you please—"

"Shh." Calla placed a finger over her lips. "You'll wake your sister." Addie was asleep in her crib.

"Sorry." Elliot and I retreated as silently as possible. Erma and Jude were still gone, so we couldn't ask them. "Oh, no. I forgot about Plink. We left her in the attic." I said.

We ran back to the attic, and I freed Plink from the cage. Once free, Plink began to dance on top of the codes, which we had left on top of the chest.

Elliot began to mimic Plink's dance, moving his hands up and down as Plink flapped her wings. "She's trying to tell us something."

Plink stopped dancing and touched her beak to the blue lock, then the orange lock, and finally the brown lock. Over and over, blue, orange, brown. Blue, orange, brown.

"I think we had it wrong all along," Elliot said.

"These aren't the right codes?"

"The codes might be right," Elliot said, "but I don't think we need to punch them in at the same time. I think we need to punch them in the right order."

Plink stopped touching the locks.

"Let's try it." I kneeled in front of the chest. "The blue one first, right, Plink?" Plink didn't peck my hand. I think that meant yes.

I punched in the blue code. The keys stayed down. "Plink," I said, "you're a genius." Plink chirped her approval.

"It makes sense," Elliot said. "The blue bird was the prototype. It was made first."

"The orange one was used for testing," I said, "so it was probably made second."

"And the brown bird was used in the war, so it was made last," Elliot said.

I entered the code into the orange lock. Like the blue one, the keys stayed down.

"Here goes nothing." I entered the brown code into the final lock. I tried to lift the lid. "It's too heavy."

"Let me help," Elliot said.

Together we slowly opened the chest. Inside was a single object. I reached in and took it out. It was a book with a well-worn cover.

"Aww, it's just some old book." Elliot shrugged. "My dad owns hundreds of those."

I began turning the pages.

"Does it have any pictures?" Elliot asked.

"A few," I said, "but mostly words."

"I was hoping we'd find another robot." Elliot searched the chest, nearly toppling into it. "Like Plink, but bigger. Maybe a clockwork dog. Or a dragon."

"This isn't just any old book," I said. "Grandfather wrote it. I recognize his handwriting." Plink perched on my shoulder. "This is better than a robot."

Elliot smiled. "If you're happy, I'm happy." He stood up and brushed dust off his pants. "This was fun, but big books aren't my thing. I think I should be going now. Research projects on toilets don't write themselves, you know."

I remembered that I had a lot to do for my project as well.

24 CONCERNING DRAICOT

I flopped onto my bed and opened Grandfather's journal. Plink sat on my pillow, surrounding herself with a fluffy white nest. Grandfather had a lot to tell about the Last War. Scattered amongst the stories were sketches of both people and machines. I recognized some of them thanks to photos I had seen in history books. I recognized the names of some battles too. Then I came across the name Draicot. I said it aloud. Plink chirped.

Professor Twain had mentioned him. I read the title of the entry: "Concerning Lieutenant General Draicot." I started reading it from the beginning. Grandfather had such nice handwriting.

The fighting was brutal at Fog Lane, but I had come to expect nothing less from Lieutenant General Draicot. Draicot was famous for his brilliant strategies as well as his cruelty. Fog Lane was my fourth time facing him. I lost a lot of good men that day. I found their bodies after the fight. I also gathered the injured as well as damaged machinery. It didn't matter if they were from Thauma or Oreshaffe. I salvaged them all.

I wasn't expecting to find Draicot. He was in sorry shape, a hole in his chest. Yet despite his condition, he did not call for help. When I approached, he pointed his gun at me. The soldier accompanying me wanted to kill Draicot on the spot, but I commanded the lad to hold his fire.

I presented Draicot with a choice: he could surrender to me, and I would do everything I could to help him, or he could remain on the field and perish. At first he was reluctant. I had to nearly beg him to surrender. In retrospect, I suppose that his surrender would require a great deal of faith in me. After all, the man had taken a bullet to the heart. Could I really save him?

Eventually Draicot did surrender. He lowered his gun. I had my companion retrieve it. Then I took Draicot into my arms and carried him to my camp. I left my fellow soldier to continue searching the battlefield.

I took Draicot to the medical tent. You see, not long ago I had completed a clockwork heart. During the war I designed more than weapons. These projects kept me sane.

I hadn't yet used the heart because there had not been the need. This was the first opportunity I had. It was a complicated procedure, and my anesthetic was not nearly as effective as the kind we have today, but Draicot endured the pain without complaint. When I was done, I had replaced Draicot's heart with a heart of my own creation.

You know the rest of the story. He has been by my side ever since. After the war, I told him he could go anywhere, and, wouldn't you know it, he chose to stay with me.

If he's alive, I imagine he's still serving my family. And assuming he is, don't worry about how skinny he is. He's always been like that. My wife and I have tried to fatten him up. We don't want anyone thinking we're trying to starve our butler. But some things don't change, I suppose.

He's the best butler I've ever had. Perhaps you'd say he's too good. He's extremely meticulous about cleaning. He's always punctual too—perhaps because he has a clockwork heart. And for whatever reason, he insists that books be stacked vertically on the shelf. I am of the opinion that you can fit more books on the shelf if you stack them horizontally, but Jude can't stand that. He always rearranges them vertically. Oh, well, I don't mind accommodating some of his quirks.

Please be good to him. He may seem callous, but I assure you he's one of the most faithful people you're likely to meet. Once he risked his life for my little son, who had foolishly slipped past the nanny to play on the thin ice over the lake. The ice broke, and my son fell into the freezing water.

Cold weather isn't good for Jude's heart. Please don't ask him to shovel snow. I always ask one of the other servants to handle that. Or I do it myself. (It's the perfect excuse to start a snowball fight, which is the only kind of fight I enjoy.) But despite the risks to himself, Jude jumped into the freezing water that day to rescue my child. My boy probably wouldn't have made it as far as he has without Jude around.

Now, Jude, if you happen to be the one reading this, thank you. I know you dislike inefficiency and sentimentality, so I shall leave it at that. And I suppose that after everything we've been through together, words aren't necessary to express what you mean to me. Farewell, my friend.

Below Grandfather had signed off as *Nick Newton*. I had never known that he had signed his name that way. In the history books he was always General Newton or the famous inventor Nicholas Newton or something along those lines.

I closed the journal. It all made sense: why Jude didn't want to talk about the Last War, why he was unsettled by Solomon's cannon when we had toured Volk Enterprises, why he made that ticking sound even when he wasn't carrying his watch.

"Plink," I said, "I've got an idea." I sat up and placed the journal carefully on my bedside table. Plink climbed up my arm and perched on my shoulder. We went down to the foyer, where there stood a small table. A few books and old framed photographs decorated the top. I moved aside the bookends, which were shaped like eagles, and stacked the books horizontally.

I heard footsteps approaching and hid behind the coat rack. It was filled with coats. Jude came by. He immediately took notice of the books. He made a sound of disapproval and reached out his hand as if to correct the horizontal atrocity. Then he paused, smiled, and instead reached out and picked up one photograph amidst all the rest. He placed the picture on top of the horizontal books and went off to attend to other duties. Plink and I came out of hiding. We looked at the photograph and saw that it was a picture of Grandfather.

NICK THE GENIUS

A few days later, Solomon, Elliot, and I were in the school library discussing the finding from the attic.

"A journal?" Solomon said. "I was hoping for a robot."

"Yeah, me, too," Elliot said.

"It's a very interesting journal," I said. "Grandfather tells stories about the Last War."

"I would be interested if it had information about the mechanical heart," Solomon said. "I'm still hoping to get one for my collection."

I shifted uncomfortably in my seat. How could I tell Solomon that Jude was using the mechanical heart? Would Solomon still want to buy it? I tried not to think about that. I didn't say anything more about the journal. "Well, I've got to get going." I stood up. "I told Jude I'd only stay for a little bit after school."

When I got home, I went straight up to my room and opened Grandfather's journal. I was already at the last chapter. As I lay on my bed, I turned to where I had left off. Plink sat on my head, peering down at the pages. I had been reading about a lot of unfamiliar names. And then I saw Plink. The drawing was very small in the corner of the page.

The clockwork bird is, in one sense, merely a toy. It flies. It sings. It follows you around. It's simply fun to have. It's also an attempt to use my military technology for other applications. But the bird is not for me. I took it apart and put it away.

I would like to be remembered for making wonderful things, but I'm afraid I've already made too many weapons. Yes, people say that I won the war with the weapons I invented and the brilliant strategies I devised. They think I'm a hero. But weapons are not wonderful things, only unfortunate realities.

In the time I have left, I have decided to focus on my medical inventions. The prosthetic arm, I'm afraid, was not a success and only resulted in more suffering. But I must try to make progress. I will leave the clockwork bird for someone else, someone who will strive after wonderful things.

Yours truly,
Not "General."
Not "genius."
Just "Nick Newton" will do.
Because that's all I am and ever hope to be.

"Me, too," I said. "Me, too."